The Ocofillo Review

Volume 5 Number 2
Summer 2021

LOVE

LUST

LONGING

fiction - poetry - truth

KALLISTO GAIA PRESS

EDITORIAL STAFF
Tony Burnett Managing Editor
Nancy Cook Flash Fiction
Mary Day Long Creative Nonfiction
Jan Rider Newman Fiction
Rod Carlos Rodriguez Poetry

BOARD OF DIRECTORS
A R (Russell) Ashworth President
Andrea Barbosa Director
Joseph Borden Director
Anthony Burnett Executive Director
Jerica Glover Secretary
Gogi Hale Treasurer
Tate Lewis-Carroll Interim Director
Mary Day Long Interim Director

ISSN: 2573-4113
ISBN: 978-1-952224-08-9
Front cover photo: Mary Day Long

© 2021 Kallisto Gaia Press Inc.
a 501(c)3 literary nonprofit
1801 E. 51st Street
Suite 365-246
Austin TX 78723

This publication is made possible, in part, by the
**City of Austin TX
Cultural Arts Division**

Table of Contents
POETRY

FICTION

TRUTH

REVIEWS

CONTRIBUTORS

* *may include passages containing graphic depictions of violence or sexual acts.*

Dear Precious Reader,

Once again, we bring some of the world's most profound scribes to play in our literary garden. As with all our previous summer issues this collection is thematic. Having been sequestered by the dasterdley Covid 19 virus for what often seems a lifetime, we feel the desire to deal with the desire; those strong subcutaneous emotions that drive our head, heart, and hormones. We dubbed The Ocotillo Review Volume 5.2 as our Love, Lust, and Longing issue. When you toss a topic with such powerful energy into the mix you have to be ready to step up. The Kallisto Gaia Press' editorial staff are neither shy nor reserved but we did have what one of our editors referred to as *doozies*. Yes, I had to look it up. We took the best of the rather hefty batch of soul-stirring stories and poems, brushed off any dust and here we present them for your reading pleasure.

There are a few pieces that may stir your prurient interest. There's also a healthy helping of platonic love, longing in its many heart-rending forms, and of course the inevitable lust that brings this issue its PG-13 rating. As always, the poets and writers we feature perform their craft with elegance, expertise, and empathy. Throw off the covers and open your hearts. Prepare to laugh, cry and possibly perspire as you enjoy what I feel is our best issue since the legendary "End of life in the age of technology" edition, from back in 2018. Note: I may be mentioning that because I found a case of those last month when I was rearranging my office. Let me know if you want a copy.

Speaking of backstock, this is our first issue where we will be using a print-on-demand supplier. If it works according to plan, we will never have another sold out issue, or boxes of backstock filling up my closet.

You are the reason we continue to put these words together in this appealing format. We are grateful for your support. Your contributions and purchases are what makes it possible to PAY our contributors, yes, with actual money, a rarity in the Lit Mag universe. If you agree that paying for art is the right way to do it, remember all contributions to Kallisto Gaia Press are 100% tax deductible. Grants are getting smaller and harder to find. If you can toss us a buck or two we will be eternally grateful. In any case, I hope you enjoy this offering.

PEACE!

Tony Burnett

Cemetery

I was just wondering
if it was safe to visit
the cemetery
feed the dead
clear the brush of loneliness
plant one more memory
in the soil?
And, of course, to talk!
Compare notes on
invisible enemies
ask a lot of questions.
Because I know
they will tell me,
It's a kindness the dead
bestow upon us
without asking for anything
in return,
except for a few flowers
and a little water to keep them alive.
If I could reach
the right cemetery
I would save a little water
for myself.

- Jasmina Wellinghoff

The Ocotillo Review

Volume 5.2

Love
Lust
Longing

Kallisto Gaia Press

Fantasy Tactics

Gliding like a camera jib, the second hand advances, passes the hour and the minute. Its smooth revolutions tracking the action, it returns and repeats the circuit... This is how we learn to touch type.

A vibrating chameleon strikes to catch a fly. I jerk awake.

"He wins the Oscar for the most monotonous voice."

Surely with those glasses, he is the Clark Kent of instructors.

Desperate, I undress his unremarkable frame, first the obligatory mask, then his jacket and tie. He offers no resistance--a seasoned actor playing his part. On a roll, I remove his belt, jeans, and faded check shirt. He stands unruffled in shorts, socks, and scarf, still spooling words. A hesitation--should I? Now near-naked, he walks to the radiator to turn up the heat, his pale backside perter than I imagined. Thankfully, he wraps his neckwear about his waist; it dribbles pathetically over his nether region.

The head of department strides in. Shocked to see him in such attire, she demands an immediate explanation. He changes the subject to his sabbatical. She proffers her tweed number, which is tight around his shoulders but at least keeps off the chill.

He blathers on, as one by one our eyes focus on infinity.

This man spends his nights on superhero duty.

His mobile rings. I forgot to take it out of his trouser pocket. It's the main unit, filming in San Francisco. Where is he? He's holding everyone up. I cover for him. He'll be there in ten.

I notice the alligator print on his underpants--its bulge-enhancing open jaw, the ample ball-hammock.

The motorcycle courier flies by. Makes the drop-off.

I rifle through the packet. Everything's there. I hope it fits.

The bell. I stretch. He winks at me and I sling him the new suit.

-*Lee Nash*

Roses

Take a picture with your phone.
Increase the saturation and send them
to the woman you met at the rally
whom you haven't had the courage to call.
Text a pithy note and add an innocent emoji,
the one with big glasses and smiling teeth.
Then send those same roses to the woman
from the association wine tasting who suggested
that you and she try the new Mongolian restaurant
(you declined; it might require chopsticks).
If you had their numbers you could send those roses
to the hygienist who cleaned your teeth yesterday
and to the dark-eyed poet who writes at the café.
Isn't this so much easier, and cheaper,
snapping roses in the park and tapping them
to faceless recipients, than that June afternoon
before the last day of seventh grade
when you loaded your pocket with change,
rode your bike to the florist on Newington Road
and picked the reddest rose in the cooler
for the girl you had a crush on since kindergarten?
The rose you never gave her, embarrassed
by the penmanship trembling on the card.

- Barry Peters

Inspector

he'd prefer it if the children were out of the way...
putting their sentiments first

he'll need a stiff drink when he gets off the *TGV*

his back's ramrod but I'm round-shouldered

I loosen his tie with a look and he says let's go to bed

I'm prepared for this – my pomegranate candle,
my bed unusually presentable

but not for the chill in his steel-
green eyes as our bodies lock

the clatter of a slender-legged kudu
as it topples on the chest of drawers

he's already destroyed my confidence by email,
painting the phenomenal ex; by phone, only talking
about himself

now he does it physically

he tells me he'd normally
walk around naked – can he do this here?

makes salmon lasagna – reads Peter Høeg
as I search for my chicest second-hand skirt

he knows what *merisier* is, of course

I don't find him avuncular

he asks for a cloth to wipe up the drops of water
from the bathroom counter

You're hopeless

it's all about his four children,
and his ex's incredible children, and money

he doesn't drive (though he won't tell me why),
so I ferry him back to the station

he says he'll be back in a month –
maybe, if his schedule permits it

as he finds his seat in the carriage
I catch him smile, not to me

at first I think it's a gesture to a stranger

then I see he's laughing to himself, mocking me
standing alone on the platform, waving

now he's had his dirty weekend,
his distraction, his low-budget fornication,
he's got to get back to Paris to work

he bought me a present, flashed his plastic –
the kids will enjoy it

it's over because you're old,
she said – she was younger by twenty-two years

driving home, I think of other reason

my nails catch the light, my first ever manicure –
not a total waste of gloss...
at least part of me didn't touch him

-Lee Nash

The Wall

Alfredo stood in the shadowy bushes on our side of the river, stroking his newly-shaven chin.

"I don't know, Manuel...we've come all this way—but how can we get past that?"

"That" was the recently-constructed barrier rising fifty feet into the sky. No chain-link fence we could climb and be done with it. No concrete wall we could tunnel beneath without being seen digging from the other side. Not even the closely-spaced bars that had replaced the chains along many sections of the border.

This barrier was a shimmering blue energy field—the latest in technological marvels—humming to itself. As we watched, a rabbit darted into it...with a crack and a flash, it was gone.

We fled together from a country that treated our relationship as a sin against nature and God. Getting this far had taken three months of walking. We shaved our beards and let our hair grow long, stealing women's clothing to wear—rumor said it would give us a better chance of passing the border...

I hugged him tightly. "We must try, *querido*. We can never go home. I'd die sooner than have them separate us."

I felt his hand stroke my hair. "You're right. We've come so far..."

We wrapped shawls around our heads, covering the lower halves of our faces, and hand-in-hand, we walked toward the barrier.

There was one opening, and it bristled with armed guards.

"Do you have papers?" growled a heavy-set sergeant.

With trembling hand, I held out the carefully-forged documents.

He scanned the pages quickly, then nodded to a subordinate.

"These seem to be in order. Take them to the women's camp."

And just like that, we were free. With all of Mexico spread before us.

-Rie Sheridan Rose

Rabbit with Cherries

I rubbed bits of moss off the soles
of my shoes to trace your name
with my finger in the cave at Lascaux.
It was a crime against eternity,

but we weren't godless louts;
we worshipped the monkey god
Hanuman, who searched the Himalayas
for herbs to save the wounded Lakshman.

Finding many, not knowing which
would work, he lugged a whole mountain
all the way across India. I'd hoped
our love would prove so tenacious,

a thing I could pound a nail into, a shield
we could float on when the waters rose
above our shoulders, a jasmine canopy
to shade us from summer's burn.

A still life, Lapin aux Cerises, hung
in our hotel bedroom, a dead hare
strung up by its hind legs, cherries
spilling around it like evening stars.

- Don Hogle

Goodbye

I know that when you put your shirt on, you have to leave. I could've stayed for hours locked between your arms, your hand gently kneading my breast as your chest hair brushes against the contours of my spine. I count the light imprints of your kisses left on my shoulders, knowing that their number is finite in the allotted time we have. Even though you dress, I stay naked, swaddled in the comforter to prolong the moment as it slips by; time is fleeting, seconds ending just as they begin, grasping at the moments before they dissipate. The toastiness of your body's protective blanket over me falls to a chill in the winter air as my body prepares for the bleak onset of loneliness.

You lean over to kiss me but I catch your face in my hands like an autumn leaf. I could let go if your eyes were not so earnest a blue. Tears gather in the creases of my eyes as I memorize your cheekbones; your skin becomes the parchment for the words retelling the time we spent together, and I run my fingertips over the prints of the stories you will take with you. It is our last few minutes in this space together before you leave; I may or may not butcher myself in madness to appease my darkness-seeking mind, committing the parting to a liminal space between forever or only a month apart. I know only my mind in the moment, and I cannot foresee even the next, let alone tomorrow. So I must commit you to my heart in case we must wait until the end of forever, and so must you.

It was never that I did not love you enough, only that the suffering was so great that a single word of any memory as solace could not break apart the leaden fog that shielded my broken mind from sunlight. But the impressions of your body remain with me still upon my skin and will go with me to the grave, those kind impressions that buffed out the welts of abuse. I will go saintly and purified from your warmth, even in death; the narratives we wove together are tattooed upon me in languages of love.

Your desire to protect me from myself makes the tears spill faster, knowing how much suffering my suicide would bring you. I tear at myself in frustration that death was all too possible, that I could not be better for you. I try all I can, holding your devotion in desperation as my own tempests rage within, despite the perfect stillness I wear for you. I try not to be swept away from you, but I cannot guarantee my strength. Now is the time for good-byes, just in case. Now is the time to make your memories, seal my face within the preservation of this moment. I'll call my doctor and stay in others' company just as I promised you, but let's not pretend that we have a "next time" committed to certainty; the only tragedy greater than my death would be to die without you knowing how much I love you and always will, even in hell, even in other lifetimes.

I'm dressed now too, seeing you to the door. You kiss me again, the last time, before you head to your car in the darkness and drive home. Maybe next time, maybe not. I let the moment dissolve as your tail lights grow faint in the night; memories are all I have now, hopefully enough to last an eternity.

-Kaitlin Kan

It was, my cousin said on the phone, "the end of an era." Howard was an intellectual, an academic. My brother used to say that speaking with Howard often made him think that he should be taking notes. The era ending event was my mom's death; Howard's call was one of condolence.

Howard went no further regarding the concept of era's end but I thought I understood what he meant. Now, though, I wish I had discussed it with him further. Howard being Howard, he likely would have brought me to places and ideas unexpected but he died just a few years later. So I am left to ponder the phrase, and his meaning, myself.

The end of an era. My mom was the last of her generation. My dad as well as my mom's siblings were already dead, all uncles and aunts gone, so too that generation's cousins. It was simple to think that was Howard's meaning. End of a generation, end of an era.

Now I think it was more than that. She was not simply the last of the family's generation, she was the link to a different time, when family lived in the same community and life itself seemed simpler. The 1950s, a time of weekend afternoon visits to see uncles and aunts, to play with cousins. Shopping for the week's food at a variety of stores, the butcher, the grocer, the fruit and vegetable guy, the baker. Riding the bus downtown for an afternoon movie. An era when large holiday dinners with extended family was a normal practice, a routine both comfortable and unquestioned.

That time ended long ago as cousins became adults and moved to faraway coasts while uncles and aunts retired and moved to warmer climes. I think, though, that my mom was more than simply a link to a time long passed and that the ended era was the conclusion of a continued tradition she maintained for half a century more.

It was the dinners, her dinners. My mom loved to entertain her family, she loved the party. Decade after decade she welcomed the chance to gather family together. An uncle and aunt, or a cousin, might visit and all within reach were summoned to dinner. On holidays even more would come and though she was never able to gather the entire family together simultaneously, at one time or another all returned and sat at her table.

Her table would be beautiful and immaculately set, of course, but it was the food she served; course after course, huge quantities, and all homemade. Even into her eighties, considerably slowed by progressive disease, she hosted these gatherings, still serving as much food as ever.

"She becomes a different person when it comes to these dinners," my dad told me in the last years of their lives when she pointedly refused his advice to "slow down a bit." She prepared everything from appetizer to dessert. Dessert. In the 1950s she began to serve what at first seemed like an exotic dish, the Jello mold. It was prepared in a large fluted form and then removed and placed on a decorative plate, a red colored gelatin with pieces of fruit – maraschino cherries, mandarin oranges, pineapple chunks – suspended in it, seemingly defying gravity. With modest ceremony at the end of the dinner she brought it out to the praise of the assembled and cut sections which were placed one by one on dessert plates and passed to each of us.

After a few years it ceased, for me, to be a welcome sight. Jello, a faux food without substance that slid around the plate and fell apart when one tried to pick up a spoonful or worse, a forkful. What about the other desserts that my mom would sometimes serve, baked goods or sweets, did we have to make it through the jello mold first? The first time I ever heard my mom curse, I many years an adult by then, was after a family dinner when she realized she had forgotten to serve the jello mold. Even into the twenty first century my mom continued to serve that relic of the mid twentieth. It had gradually become a parody of itself and its absence at the end of one dinner a cause of genuine disappointment for us all.

Jello or not, those dinners were wonderful times as family would sit around the table, enjoy the reunion, recount the latest news and recall earlier happenings while my mom would look out over her table, her guests, her family, and hold court, asking questions and offering opinions, giving advice and encouraging us to please have more to eat.

It may be easier nowadays to keep in touch, e-mail, cellphones, internet but that era of family, of warm and comfortable times when we gathered and spent time together face to face, which my mom continued for decades, provided a far more tangible and enjoyable connection.

So it was the end of an era as there is no one else to summon, to gather, to orchestrate in the insistent way she did. Family gathered once more, one final time, upon her passing, traveling from distant coasts south and west, and from the other side of the world, and we all sat at her table and had more to eat to mark the era's end.

-Harvey Silverman

A Bicycle Built for Two
Editor's Choice - Flash Fiction

He tipped his hat, a bowler, brown like the wet sand, and a perfect complement to his navy wool jacket and tweed trousers. She smiled at him, the smile of his dreams, and offered him a gift wrapped in birthday paper and blue ribbons. He opened it and saw a book of poetry and was pleased. He slipped it into his breast pocket and gave it a pat over his heart. She smoothed her pink crinoline petticoats and peeked up at him under lowered eyelids. The sweetheart neckline of her dress teased his senses and he could smell her scent as it waft over him.

She took his arm and enjoyed the roughness of the jacket fabric against her skin. They walked down the boardwalk, he in spats and she in kitten heels, alternately slapping and pinging away at the wooden slats. The waves of the ocean kept time with their cadence, a backdrop of blue with white foam. Salt in the air awakened childhood memories of bygone days at the shore. They passed Adirondack chairs, with wooden slats painted white, under umbrellas in the sweet colors of ice creams. They passed a child drawing clouds with pastel chalk on the walkway, and came to Boardwalk Bicycle Rentals. The sign over the door was weathered by the sea, but the red, white, and blue bicycles all lined up in rows were shiny with fresh paint.

The couple went inside and rented a bicycle built for two, only for an hour, just enough time to enjoy a short ride on the boardwalk and watch the seagulls soar. He paid the clerk with one bill extracted from his brown leather wallet, soft with age and use. He
mounted the bike and held it steady for her while she climbed onto the second seat behind him and settled her dress.

He pushed off with his right foot and she with her left, the momentum propelled them for a short while. As they began to wobble, he pressed harder on the pedals and she felt her feet pulled without traction.

"Let me help," she said, trying to get her footing.

"We're not in sync," he laughed, "get on the same rhythm I've got going."

"I'm trying," she laughed too.

The front wheel spun around in harmony with the pace and details of daily life. The back wheel turned in unison acknowledging the mysteries of fate and time. The two could not quite balance the load, the weight of the couple transferring alternately to first one wheel, then the other and back again.

Magically, in one brief moment, reality and mystery met and the bicycle glided. She removed her hands from the bars and wrapped them around his waistcoat. He caressed her crossed hands on his chest with one arm while he balanced the bicycle with the other. Peace flowed and time was transcended.
A gull swooped down and blessed, then interrupted their dance.

The balance was disturbed, and the wobbling began again. He grabbed both handlebars, and she released her arms and gripped the rear set.

After a frustrating quarter mile he finally said, "Just put your feet on the pegs. I'll pedal."
"But I want to help too," she said, "We can do it."

"It's not working", he said, "just let me do it."

"It will go faster and smoother if we work together."

"That's ok, I don't mind doing it."

She gave in and he steered them round the bend and back to the rental shop. They hopped off, she smoothing her dress and he adjusting his vest while taking a peek at his pocket watch.

"You looked so beautiful on the bike," he said.

"But I was behind you, you couldn't see me."

"I could see you in my mind's eye," he said.

She pouted her lips.

So kissable, he thought. He patted his breast pocket, "Thanks again for the book."

"I hope you enjoy it. Perhaps we'll ride again next Sunday?" she asked.

"Perhaps," he said, and then gestured toward the pocket watch. "Duty calls."

They parted on the boardwalk, she in one direction, he in the other. Neither noticed the seagulls soaring. He walked until he came to his cottage of music and books, work papers and family photos. He placed a record on the phonograph and lowered the needle. The music swelled to cover the scratching of the black disc going around and around. He sat at his desk and took the book she had given him from his pocket. He opened it and started to read the first poem:

chalk on a sidewalk
marks the dreams
of a child's pure heart

a box of stained glass
held together by hopes and dreams
requires tender care

He looked around at the partially read books and all the paper to be filled and filed. He looked at the black and white pictures of his family in silver and gold frames on the desk. He closed the book.

"No, not now," he said aloud.

He pulled the wooden stepstool over to the tallest

bookshelf beside his desk and took a step up, placing the gift on a high spot.

He sank into his desk chair, smiled sadly into a photograph of his family, and stared out the window toward the blue sky, past the columns of paper, books, and rubble of life piled around him. The music once again caught his ear and mingled with the smell of her on his jacket.

-Manning Wolfe

Strip Poker in a Cabin in Montana

For every article of clothing,
reveal a different scar.

Two of a kind: Just you and me,
and the pine walls and pine floor.
Midnight creak of wood
answering snow's frosty call.
Count the rings to see a document
of past traumas. Bite mark
like a pale crescent rising
on your forearm. A moon
held in a different sky. A new mouth
now touches that burden.
Shirts piled on the woody floor.
Your body a blessing to my lips.

Ace High: Somewhere on a snow-laden meadow,
a red fox stands alone. Her mane ablaze
 like the logs in our room. A little heat.
A little triumph. The glacial remains of a canyon.

Full House: Profane, obligate, the place
where the miscarried child was carried.
Past histories spiral away from us
like sable tracks in snow. On this
uncertain earth there are so many
geysers waiting to go off.
We hold what's faithful: green eyes
in a dark room, winter thawing,
the hands we're dealt to play.

Royal Flush: Fully nude and lit
by an amber light. No winners, only lovers.

-Jordan Escobar

We Could've Been Country Kids

Out there, where phone lines snap
with messages to no one,
blue-embered sky darkens
over grapevines and heat trickles
a tannic runnel down your spine.
We could've held hands. We could've
prayed for that silence to last decades,
to spread beyond rows
of pomelo. Our thoughts might've
spiraled into erasure, grasping at
presence. This moment
of pain, you might've told me,
God doesn't love you. I might've
believed you. We might've killed
to taste each other. You might've
named me Prodigal, so I could
whisper Apocrypha. And the sky
could open, and spill its secrets.
Rain slicked and trembling
like two infants born again
in the back of a pickup, searching
for mouths, praying for ghosts
made of flesh, knowing each other
in fantasies that never existed.
On farms that never bloomed.
Fallow. Dead and dried. The drought
carried into the long years of our lives.
Alone and apart and left to ash. We could've
been north-stars. We could've been
field mice. We could've been
every flower not blossoming
in that field of unbirthed lilies.

-Jordan Escobar

Ugly

High school smells like canned corn and you thought it would be big enough to hide in, for your skin to bleed into the beige tile, walk so your feet make no sound. Make your face disappear into perfect smoothness and will your hair to be blonde, long, straight. You try. You iron the awful orange curls *God gave you. Oh,* the ladies in the salon say. *Oh, those beautiful curls. Oh how lucky.*

Fucky lucky.

You take the iron on the highest setting and you lay your head on the kitchen table and press the iron as close to your scalp as you can and push down so the steam boils the edge of your ear and afterward there will be blisters and so what.

The field is between the high school and your house. Dirt and sharp rocks, bottle caps, rusted slide. Wind kicking dust from the diamond. Gulls settled in a puddle on the blacktop. And always a group of boys.

Hey Ugly.

Head down, eyes on the ground. They make sounds like a seal or a dog and thrust their hips at you and laugh. And it's the laughing that you hear even when you're rocking yourself back and forth in bed that night and it's only the first week of high school. When you're staring at the medicine cabinet wondering how many aspirin you need to swallow to die and you stand there with the bottle and look in the mirror. Freckle face red headed bucktooth wiry Brillo hair glasses. And your little brother comes in with his lumpy face and his wet Mongoloid eyes and he strokes your face tender.

Alone in your bedroom you try to love. You love your

thighs. The freckles on your arms, the freckles on your face, the bones of your knee. You try to love everything about your body and you build a fortress around it. Your fat ankles, your pale lashes. Your teeth. You love and you promise to wait, deep inside yourself, for later—after high school sometime—when you will walk by a group of boys and no one will say anything at all. You promise that you'll wait until you grow up and you'll be beautiful then.

The field is crunchy with freeze and it's fun to walk on.
  Hey Ugly!
  The sounds.
  Hey dog!
  The pretend barking.
  And all your work at loving yourself is for nothing. Your brain turns to glass.

You don't know their names. You know their jackets: TCC sewn on the front pocket. You hear it stands for The Cock Club. The boys show up together at dances. They have steps they all know that are the same and they dance to "Papa Was a Rolling Stone."
  At homecoming you danced with your friend Lisa until a guy asked her to dance and then you sat on the bleachers in the dark and waited for it to be over and for your dad to show up to drive you home.
  You'll always be beautiful to me, he said, when you ran to his car and burst into tears.

Mother is popping pimples on your back and in between she's smoking. You're both sitting on the couch in your nightgowns and her legs are long and brown and freckle-less.
  You have to have personality or looks, so you should start working on your personality, she says.

She seems either afraid of you or tired of you.

The thought of going to school shuts you down. The thought of staying home shuts you down.

Your brother brings you a flier about a thing. His gift to you. They need kids. Some Halloween mansion. Your mother rolls her eyes. Because she rolls her eyes you go. And because your brother.

You sit with other kids in a fake mansion. They talk you through what you signed up to do. They show you where you stand. Hide in a secret pocket in a hallway. Hear people coming toward you. Wait until they've gone past you. Jump out and hit a metal bucket with a crowbar. Scare them so they piss themselves.

They give you a black cape.

They give you a crow mask.

In the parlor with a pipe.

The dark you see with your eyes closed is the same dark you see when you open them. You suck in sweet rubber of your mask. Adjust to gray-on-gray, fake cobwebs against chipped drywall. Load your greedy eyes with dark, your ears with buzzers, your nose with chainsaw smoke. A kid comes around the corner, a stripe of red exit sign light scissoring across his neck.

The crowbar's weight in your hand feels adult.

School is endless. The field is dark when you cross it.

Hey, Ugly.

A cat call. Then they're in front of you, surrounding you. They make kissing sounds. You take a step. They block your way. You look at the ground. You smell the sweat stink of wool baseball jackets.

Fuck you. You say it out loud.

They laugh. One pushes you into another. *Kiss*

her. That one pushes you back. *You kiss her.*

Fuck you all. You yell it.

One holds your arms and you kick at the one that's grabbing for your foot. Then four of them are holding you and they pin your shins and arms to the ground and the ground is tight under your back and the grass cracks under your elbows and you need to be gone from here. Now is a flicker of a lime street light. Now is a sparrow in the dusk. You are grass you are dirt you are asphalt pebble leaf. But they don't do anything but hold you down. They don't know what to do next. You are all too young for this.

Despite everything you know and hate, you suck in your stomach.

You feel

Every second

You see

The crease in the jeans cuff beside your head

Ketchup on the t-shirt sleeve holding you down

Grass stain on the knuckle

Rip on the rubber sole of a sneaker.

Her lips are chapped, one says. *She's been busy.*

They laugh.

You don't know what it means. They're not sure what it means.

They release your arms and legs.

Let's get out of here.

And they go, forgetting you.

You feel your own body's weight on the ground and the tickle of wet grass under your ass. You tug your skirt down to cover your knees.

What did you expect the grass whispers.

You get up and lean against a tree. You are cold under your skirt. The wind moves the swings. You walk home. Tomorrow perches on the edge of each roof lining your street, one hand on its crotch, the other picking at your hair with a fingernail.

In your room you glue yourself back together. You swallow back your guts. Feel your arms attached to trunk, feet to floor. Calm your heart, your heart, your heart.

Your father calls up to your room: *dinnertime, beautiful.*

You don't want to go but he drives you to the mansion. *It's the last night*, he says. *Halloween!*

You are glad for your corner of dark, you feel safe in the world inside the world. Bird mask, wet breath. Fake torches, headless dolls, painted blood. Your stiff red curls snake out along the drywall and disappear into the poisonous vines painted there. You disturb the gentle clouds of fake fog with your hand. Shadows of kids slide along the walls like horses. They slip across ceilings.

You see their jackets round the corner, maroon washed to gray in the dark.

Crow bar in your hand. How your fingers itch.

How you clutch the bar in both hands. You raise it high. Your shadow scales the wall. It is enormous. The dark is nervous around you.

(Would anyone blame you?)

You bang the bar on the can. One turns.

You want to be seen.

You smile under your mask.

Then you hear it. From another part of the mansion, a man-goat sound. You know who and why and your heart panics. You drop the bar, the mask. Run along the fake walls, claw apart seams, feel your way through the dark to your brother. Snot running down his chin. Crouched in a corner, arms wrapped over his head, flabby bare belly showing. Scared. Kids cluster and you hiss, *Get lost.* You wrap your brother in your cape and you talk to him, tell him it's not real, lead him out of the mansion to the street and the light.

Your dad, waiting. Apologizing: *Your brother wanted to see you. I thought he'd like it. I didn't realize it would scare him. I didn't know.*

You sit on the curb and stroke your brother's head whispering, *It's alright, it's just pretend. We're okay. See?*

He settles, leans against you. You lead him to the car. Dad holds the door open for him, takes him home.

You go back to your pocket in the dark.

Bang the bar. The sound hollows you and fills you.

The night is over. You leave the cape, mask in the make-up trailer . Some kids—evil nurse girl, Leatherface, scary doll girl—passing a joint in its shadow.

Hey crow!

You stop.

That was awesome, what you did tonight.

With that retarded kid.

Very cool.

Totally cool.

You coming to the cast party, they say. Your insides seize. They walk, as if you'd join. You do. You go. You dance. "Ain't No Mountain High Ain't No Valley Low." You smoke pot. You feel. You float. When you walk home the pavement sparkles with frost. Your lungs are full like when you break through the surface of a lake and gulp the air, so sudden and so bright. Tomorrow winks from the rooftop as you slide by.

Your brother is asleep on the couch with the TV on. You lift his heavy head onto your lap and trace the shape of his beautiful eyebrows with your finger and you pray that this is a night you'll remember always.

-Lesley Bannatyne

27

To the Poet on Page Twelve

I imagine you at a reading of your new book
The words shaping your mouth
in positions of *lick, lust, earlobe*

I could fall into those positions
Suck you into the well where you want to drink
But you live out East and I'll never hear you read

So instead I throw my panties on the page
Isn't that what you really want, dream about
Poet rock star status

All I'd have to do is tell a few gossips
how those panties were ripened with your words
And you'd make Facebook all over the world

Your book sales would soar
Women would shop at Victoria's Secret
Bathe and put on make-up before reading that night

But I'd have to tell them that on page sixteen
you shaped creepy crawly words, like *spider*
The one you put in your sister's dresser drawer

Hoping it would wind up inside something she wore
Like on this tremble of skin
Itchy now and swollen by the slap on page twenty

Where you can't quite position the shape of *ass*
Spiders could have their sex appeal
But a rock star would never mold the words *gluteus maximus*

-*Ellaraine Lockie*

Kiki

I was really looking forward to the event, since I hadn't been to a party in years—not since the pandemic started. Kiki, as she was known to us, her billions of followers, was scheduled to come online at three-twenty that day, and I'd scheduled my break in advance. Three months in advance, to be exact. Then, like the spontaneous rock star she is, Kiki rescheduled it for three-forty, which meant I had exactly six minutes to celebrate, though who was I to complain?

So, there I was in my home-office-cubicle, headset mounted, champagne glasses raised (I'd saved one for Spike, my Chihuahua), the Mumm bottle ready to pop. Yes, it was nonalcoholic, though I'd upped my dose of Procentra, and I was ready to have a good time. I even threw on my favorite party dress—a sleeveless lace floral, which wasn't distasteful but still had some flare—and my favorite Ralph Lauren heels, which were a pain to walk around in. Not that I walked.

It was then that I got the strange message. The news flashed across the screen that Kiki Eldorado, the International Poet Laureate, Grammy-Winning Vocalist, Media Sensation, Acclaimed Actress and Model and Youth Voice, was dead at age twenty-two, the victim of an apparent drug overdose. The whole world was bracing to mourn.

I took off my headset gracefully, set down my glass, and examined Spike's panting face. He was mournful, to be sure, but still flustered by the looks of it, as if he couldn't quite fathom her death.

"How is this possible?" he barked.

I don't know, I replied, lowering the brim of my glass. I'd only been with the corporation for six months—it was a new conglomeration, amassing all existing businesses, and providing at-home product delivery, as well—and I thought I'd seen it all in that time: bosses come and go, citizens' revolts, Third-World pleas for independence, dog suffrage. None of it materialized. Profit margins soared. Food prices fell. And I admit the home-procurement was great, not that I craved my independence much, truthfully—though I often wonder what it would be like to go outside, as I guess people used to do before lockdowns.

What I still can't fathom is the fact of her doing it. Ending her life. Just like that. It's been about eleven months since The Incident. Try as I might, I can barely recall her gleaming face—all images of her have been dutifully wiped. Yet I still hear the sounds of her poems, which she recited at least twice at livestreamed events: once during the Superbowl Halftime Show; another at the inauguration of our new CEO. And, of course, who can forget the bootlegged edition of her impassioned pleas to the Chairman of the Board and his friends, along with their sponsors, on their yacht outside Davos in '26. I still recall the sounds of her words: *Change. Change comes easily. It breathes like a bird. It flies, soars, crescendos. It speaks.* The words sent a flutter back then, a shrill beat, through my heart.

"You've gotta get back to work", Spike replied. He was chewing on appendages, possibly a child's.

What I wouldn't give now to have Kiki's lost voice.

-Joshua Bernstein

Instinct for Touch

We wake. The owls
        convulse the woods below.
    Stiff as possums,
we lie on a rummaged
        mattress, the screened
            porch our answer
    to April's early swelter.
Their bellows, hoots,
        call and response,
            their instinct for touch—
    like our bodies,
sleep's arrival, even
        in heat's ruthless press,
            sheathed in barest gauze,
        brush of sheet on skin.

    And we long to touch
            the dead, loft words
        to dormant ears,
voices to clouds
        beseeching rain,
            its graze, thunder,
        its burst, antiphonal
rumble from the other
        side. We are owls
            coveting the dark
        echo of our need,
naked slumberers
        reaching for cover.

-Annette Sisson

Hunger and Thirst

I was 16.
In theory, a Mormon girl growing up in decadent 1970s Los Angeles would enjoy knowing boys in her own religion, boys who wouldn't offer her cocaine or expect her to have sex. But my relationship with the boys at church, most of whom I had known since I was about three, was rocky. When we were children, they'd snipe at me and I'd snap back at them. By the time we were teenagers, the decade-long spat had escalated to toxic taunting. I dreaded the time I was required to be where they were.

That Tuesday night, the boys were shambling around the door I'd have to walk through to leave. As I walked their way, the ringleader called out, "Here comes the evil troll!" The other boys laughed. He went on, mocking me for being short and fat, his lip curling as he yelled that my mother was a fat cow. More laughs. I put down my head and walked out of the church.

But what tore down to the very bottom of my heart wasn't what he said. It was something much worse: it was the piercing, mortifying truth that I still wanted him to like me. He was tall, blond and smart. I had a crush on him, not because he was kind, or funny, or because he saw or valued me, but because he was my pack's alpha, the most desirable boy in the room. Despite his contempt, I wanted him to like me.

Was my judgement so easily corrupted by my hormones? Was I going to spend my life wanting the wrong men for the wrong reasons just because I was female? Had I thrown my dignity away without even realizing it? Would I be able to get it back?

When I finally made it home, even my bedroom wasn't enough of a refuge; I shut myself in my bedroom closet. My mother heard and tried to comfort me, but I sent her away. Grief, humiliation, and fear merged in me into something so painful and hopeless that I could not speak. I could only sob.

I was 22.

I had skipped the normal rites of teenagerhood—the delights and mishaps of sex, drinking, and drugs. I'd been obedient. I'd played it safe. But as a young woman starting a career and life in Manhattan, I wanted to learn at least *something* about men and myself. I hated feeling like a goldfish, huge eyes and cheeks puffed out as I took in the world outside of my bowl, trapped in my obvious and incurable separateness by my religion.

At dinner with one of my guy friends from work, I brought up my situation. My friend, who knew I was Mormon, said he would teach me anything I wanted to learn about men and sex, within whatever limits I set. Safe exploration was a requirement, because I was expected to be a virgin bride. And so we began.

Hookups are ubiquitous for normal young people in their twenties, but I wasn't a normal young person and I wasn't hooking up. I was building a platform on the lip of my goldfish bowl, inching away from how I was expected to live toward something new.

After I built some confidence, I started to experiment with other boys I met—without sex of course. For the most part, I found delight and a delicious power in the time I spent with them. There were a few encounters that felt threatening or disrespectful, but they were rare. In the main, I learned to have fun, to feel carbonated by my hormones, to enjoy being a woman in a body.

The fun, delight, and power were heady new feelings for me. But I knew that I hadn't learned everything, that I hadn't succumbed to how I might feel and who I might become with a man I loved.

I was 24.

I loved living in New York City. Lanford Wilson's *Burn This* was playing on Broadway, and I had no idea what was in store when I walked into the Plymouth Theater that night. John Malkovich and Joan Allen's tempestuous, tender love story blew up my head and my heart. Was this what a man could be like? The leonine ferocity, the sacred vulnerability, the orange pekoe tea?

It was ravishing to fall into Pale and Anna's passionate dyad. I was dazed and preoccupied on the way home, as I took off my makeup and brushed my teeth, as I put on a faded, giant t-shirt and got into bed.

There I lay, on the sofa bed in my rented room in an Upper West Side apartment, a former dining room made private by a hastily installed pressboard divider, staring at the ceiling, almost panting. I didn't know that love could be like that. (I was too carried away to remind myself that the play was *fiction*.) My heart clenched with hot rapacious hunger chilled by fear that this kind of love would never happen for me, a good Mormon girl. I thrashed in my sheets, choked by awakened, unreasonable need. It was a long night.

Not long after seeing *Burn This* I saw an Almodovar movie in which one of the characters says that she had sex so intense it made her remember being in the birth canal. *What?* I thought. *Sex can create an experience like that? What am I missing?*

I was 30.

I fell in love with a Mormon man, who, miraculously, loved me back. My every molecule breathed in optimism and possibility. We planned a December wedding.

He was killed just before Labor Day weekend.

Death doesn't negotiate. It takes without giving a damn what the taking does to you. Death slapped me across the face, pushed me down, kicked me in the stomach and then rode away without a backward glance.

People talk about a broken heart, but that's an insufficient description. Grief had torn my heart out of my chest, thrown it down on a marble slab, and whacked at it over and over again, shredding it into a pulp.

My fiancé and I never had sex. We were waiting until we got married, because that is what observant Mormons do. Yes, not having sex with a man I loved so deeply, when I was young and beautiful, is the greatest regret of my life. How could it not be?

I was 45.

I lost my virginity. To a man I'd met that morning.

Although I thought I'd learned my way around men, this was wholly new. Actual sex was all metaphor, all fact, all meaning, all sensation. There was depth and beauty in letting this man open me in this profound and yet ubiquitous way. I heard ten thousand years of women's bodies speaking through mine.

I   n the days afterwards, I felt an irrational, unslakable desire to be subject to this man I'd only met once. These feelings were beyond religion, beyond philosophy, beyond thought. Every cell in my body told me that he was the only thing that mattered in my life. I fought against these unwelcome, insistent hormones, and yet for the first time I also felt like I'd earned a place in the gorgeous, pulsating tribe of humans who know how sex can change a body.

We saw each other just one more time. I had wanted so badly to keep practicing, keep learning, keep pouring water on my desiccated soul, but no. He disappeared.

After flinging myself out of the goldfish bowl, I climbed back in and stayed there. I am not meant for casual sex.

Still, in the next decade there would be nights when I could not sequester or deny a deep, unbidden need for that magnificent masculine energy. Sometimes, when I contemplated all that I'd lost, all that I never had and why, my chosen chastity filled me with a grief and isolation that made it hard to breathe. But I could not turn my back on my religion, which inculcated in me from birth a vocabulary for the divine that suffuses every cell in my body. How could I walk away from my own soul?

I'd lie there, staring wide eyed at the ceiling, longing for a different past and a different future, feeling that unsated hunger corroding me from within.

I am 58.

Desire no longer lives inside my body like a restless, enormous animal. I watch movies and think, *Those are exceptionally attractive people,* but I don't shiver with awakened longing as they satisfy each other on screen. This diffidence, part of the inheritance of menopause, is more a relief than a loss.

For decades, my female body was a vessel—for hopes, for shame, for dogma, for fantasy, for scrutiny, for shuddering sobs, for exquisite love and thwarted desire. Now, finally, I am opening a new door. I am learning to breathe peacefully on the other side of the battles, the fears and the hopes, to become a woman who contains everything and nothing at the same time.

-Lisa Poulson

It is chilly, even for November. Drizzle clings to the skin of Hal's red Mustang. The trees, naked and bony, struggle against the wind.

"You're cold," he says, putting his arm around Donna and pulling her closer. Through the Aran knit of his sweater, she can feel his heart, a pulsing hammer. It always comes as a surprise: how real he is, how close. He kisses the rim of her ear, then lifts her hair from inside the collar of her pea coat. "Your hair," he says, his voice reverent. "It always smells so good."

Her hair, the least part of her: she grows it, she washes it—but his praise is still intoxicating. Here, in the secret darkness of his car, just the two of them, she is his girl. The one he wants.

His kisses are light and teasing, they brush against her lips and are gone. From being with him these last few months, she knows he will wait until she is ready, until she kisses him back, fully, passionately. He never hurries her, and tonight, because it is damp and chilly, and because she senses something in his mood, she dawdles, letting her mouth stray to his neck and earlobes, running her fingers over the cables of his sweater.

"Did you know that on the Aran Islands every wife has a distinctive stitch, one that is hers alone?"

"And why is that?" he asks, his hand drifting over her hair.

"That way if her husband is lost at sea, they can identify him. They'll know who he is, just by the sweater."

He pushes her hair behind her ears. "Can you knit?" he asks.

The question comes as a surprise. "Yes. My mother taught me." This is the first time he has asked her a question that seems prompted by genuine curiosity. The first time she has told him even the smallest thing about her childhood. And she longs to have him ask something else, something even more personal.

Instead, his hands drop heavily to her shoulders. "Knit me a sweater sometime and we'll see," he says, squeezing tightly. And she understands then that he is waiting.

When she offers him her mouth, it's a kind of surrender, though his lips are warm and soft and luxurious. She has the sensation, the sensation she always has, of sinking into one of her mother's eiderdowns, of being submerged in it. Then his tongue enters her mouth, and she feels as if she is melting. It would be easy—there's a secret part of her that knows this—to give herself over completely, to let him have his way, whatever that would be. There is another part, though, a not-so-secret part, which is frightened.

The Doors come on the radio, and the two of them pause, foreheads touching, eyes trained on their laps. "Come on, baby, light my fire," Jim Morrison sings, and his voice is as cool and distant as death.

"Touch me," Hal whispers.

She pulls back. "What?"

"Touch me," he says again and the small of her back goes cold.

"No," she says. "No, I couldn't."

"Just for a little, through my clothes," he coaxes, and he takes her hand, placing it where he wants it. She isn't moving, isn't breathing. It's as if she is frozen in place.

"You want to please me, don't you?" he asks, and his voice is reasonable and calm, like a parent talking to a child. She doesn't say anything, and his hand, resting on hers, starts moving up and down.

She allows this to happen, but it's as if she's watching through a window. As if her hand is separate from the rest of her body. Vaguely, she's aware of being disgusted by him. His shabby, shameful needs seem to stand in the way of something better that could exist between them, but she can't bring herself to blame him. It's the way men are. She thinks ahead to when she'll be back in her dorm room with Amy and Lisa, the three of them talking; but then, suddenly, he moans a little and pushes her hand down harder. Through the thin layer of fabric, she can feel his erection swelling, actually expanding, and then, almost as if it's alive, it gives a little leap, and she flies backward, snatching her hand away as if it's been burnt. The small of her back is jammed up against the door handle. For a long time he says nothing, just looks at her as rain pats the top of the Mustang. "It's called petting," he says. "Petting, that's all." He fumbles for a cigarette.

"You've heard of petting, haven't you, Donna?"

Feeling foolish, she watches as he taps out a cigarette, lights it and takes a deep drag. She wants to apologize, say she is sorry, redeem herself somehow, but the tears are too close to the surface. If she tries to talk, she knows that she'll cry.

"How long would you say we've been going out, Donna?" he asks, not looking at her. She doesn't answer, but he doesn't expect an answer. "About three months, right?" he says, glancing over at her quickly and then looking away when she nods. "And don't you think most guys, after that long, would be asking for a helluva lot more?"

She is alone and miserable, watching as drops of rain creep down the windshield. "I'm sorry, Hal, really I am," she says but the tears spill over into her voice and she covers her face with her hands, ashamed. She is actually crying now, head in her hands, unable to stop herself.

He smokes the cigarette halfway down, then opens the window a crack and tosses it outside. The air reaching in to her is cold and fresh.

"Okay, okay, it's all right," he says and reaches out with his arm to pull her closer. "I'm not going to make you do anything you don't want to. Donna, c'mon, please," he says. "Don't cry. You're making me feel bad." And he reaches into his back pocket and pulls out a clean handkerchief. "Here," he says, handing it to her. "Give a blow." She does as he instructs, feeling childish but safe as he kisses the top of her head.

"This is what I get for dating an eighteen-year-old," he mumbles as they pull away, but there's something in the tone of his voice that makes her think he's pleased, that he likes her this way.

-Roberta Gates

We'll Get to You Next, Janet Whiskers

7:35 AM

I can see light glowing from the back room so I know Marshall worked through the night on wedding flowers. All I hope is that he didn't fall asleep again on that rancid pile of movers' blankets…with the cat. The stubborn-ass lock finally gives and, balancing coffee, I heave open the heavy glass door. The nasal vocal stylings of Edith Piaf greet me, Edith being Marshall's go to when trying to get over someone. He definitely spent the night. It smells of yesterday in here: litterbox and Doritos, limp greens and stagnant water. Cardboard and copper fungicide. And a thin, nearly imperceptible floral perfume.

Marshall is grieving. Boyfriend moved out. In this state he tends to eat lots of sweet rolls, and obsesses over his competitors' websites deep into the night. Three days ago he adopted a cat, his fourth. The others, Marcus, Sextus, and Publius, original littermates, live in his condo. They are lumpy and old and beyond moody, no help at all. This young tabby, "Janet Whiskers", he's decided will reside full time here in the store. I've been through Marshall's rebound strategies before; this will be a new love, one easier to keep an eye on.

I don't have a problem with this workplace arrangement, but today is the day we sell our souls to make a little money, "VD", Valentine's Day, and this wiry little bit of striped fur looks to be uncomfortable, disoriented. It is expelling wretchedness in monstrous little cries that, well, I just have to say, don't sound fully animal. So now I'm thinking I might have a problem with this arrangement. And, by the way, who names a cat "Janet"? I admit seeds of annoyance have been planted under my skin.

Marshall emerges from the back room looking like hell and smelling more than vaguely like Fancy Feast. I raise a meaningful eyebrow at him before I sign in.

Sign in, 8:02 AM
Our mail carrier B.J. blows in and flings a stack of bills and promos on the counter. He stalks out, as bow legged and bitter a man as ever was. I don't believe he's ever uttered a word to us. Marshall and I have chalked it up to an all-consuming woman-hate. We exchange quick eye rolls then turn attention to the day's plan of attack.

8:15
Amazingly, Hugo is on time. Janet's prowling and huffing and mewling amuses him, despite the fact that it seems to be picking up steam. Marshall says she's simply adjusting to her new kitty surroundings. I'm grateful we haven't opened yet. He dumps more food into her pink pussy bowl, fiddles with the sound system and turns up NPR. I sift through orders. Hugo checks his Insta before beginning prep—buckets of prunus and lilac branches needing to have their woody ends smashed, hydrangeas to be soaked, regiments of stiff tulips to be rehydrated, and slicing the ends off those miserable, pesticide laden roses. Marshall needs to refocus on his bride's bouquet: subtle Saharas, pink ranunculus, and green mini cymbidiums. But sorrowful, increasingly disturbing noises are echoing off the walls. He stops to admit, irritated and apologetic, *yeah, OK, I think Janet might be in heat…*

8:26
I am sharpening my comprehension of the word "caterwauling". Also "immolation".

9:08

Crazy Jules with the Haldol-frozen face and bird nest hair
has shuffled over from the halfway house down the street
to wish us a happy St. Valentine's Day and ask for a cup of
coffee. She gives her annual shpiel about the good clergy-
man who tried to marry soldiers on the sly and paid for
it with his life when the Emperor found out. Apparent-
ly Valentine's Day was a pain in the ass from the get go.
Marshall nods as he wraps a tea rose for her and gives her
two dollars to go have a coffee across the street. On her
way out she asks if the cat is dying.

9:16

Shiree arrives and throws up in the trash can. Shiree
claims she has the flu, but I knows hangover when I sees
it. She is redirected, sent home, much to Hugo's relief.
He checks and rechecks his platform sneaks for splat-
ters. Marshall waves this little glitch off, saying we can do
without her.

9:40

While we are waving off and doing without Shiree, Mar-
shall reboots Piaf and calls Sabrina, loudly thanking God
when she says yes, she can come in.

9:45

Both phone lines are going like someone ate too many
prunes. In front, there is an accumulation of highly con-
fused customers, courtesy of Janet Whiskers' inharmoni-
ous outpouring. I distract by handing out free flowers to
some small children who have begun trying to catch the
ill-tempered kitty.

10:00

Finally in the zone. Whipping through arrangements,

Red roses, red roses, red roses…red, red, red, roses, roses…tulips, tulips, pink, red, pink…coffee, blinders….
dear god

10:03
WTF! A rosaceous little man just materialized inside our back service exit! He had to have sneaked in through the alley door. Flattened against the wall, he decided to hiss at us creepily, impressing upon us our dire need for security, that we are easy targets. We stare as he peels himself from the shadows and proudly declares he is using this brilliant strategy to sell commercial alarm systems for ADP. Marshall whips out his phone and dials 911 and the company to complain. Kicks the guy's dubiously legal ass out. We cancel 911, but yeah, we are unnerved. ADP Man will be too, when he finds he has lost that lousy job.

10:40 AM
Arguing with a customer over the phone. Explaining why we won't make out his girlfriend's enclosure card to say *Will you be my nigga* is apparently like trying to explain rocket science to a frog. What a lucky girl.

10:45 AM
Cranking out three "Tulip only" arrangements ambidextrously side by side. They really say you're somebody special, am I right? Multiple buckets jammed with spear-headed, powder pink Dutch tulips surround me. They're starting to make my throat clench, like too much sugar in lemonade. It's going to be a long-ass day, especially if that pubescent cat doesn't stop pacing and heaving forth her nasty tabby-sex come-ons. Pretty hard to believe it isn't making Marshall's skin crawl…never mind the obvious, the powerful tool it has become in repelling customers. The last three walk-ins I caught a glimpse of

looked as if they were in a dentist's chair, drill hovering.

10:58 AM
Hell and torture in the form of young feline desire echoes louder and louder off the concrete floor and brick walls of our workspace in a rhythmic, warped, bedeviled loop. The declarations of Satan through the soft, whiskered mouth of a kitty cat. Sabrina tries petting her, but Janet freaks like it's an attempt at exorcism.

11:11 AM
Hugo comes back from a "bathroom break" with eye-shadow on and a glazed donut in hand. He eats noisily while reviewing his delivery route. God I'm hungry.

11:14 AM
A phone order comes in: gerbera daisies, Mylar heart balloons, and a teddy bear. I enlighten this customer: we don't do such regalia. Ours is a more modern aesthetic, blah, blah. Before the hang up I'm told off. *Whaddaryou-guys,idiots? You're a florist, it's Valentine's day... you don't have a fuckin' teddy bear?*

      Hostility...I don't think Teddy would approve.

11:22 AM
Then again, trimming a stem of a rose I puncture my finger on a thorn and drop my knife on my foot. There is blood and cursing. Fucking Valentine roses.

11:23 AM
That's it. No more. I limp from my station. I'm on a mission to rid us of Satan's handmaiden out there. I scoop up the cat and carry her past Marshall, past the main cooler, open the door to his tiny office and unceremoniously toss her in. As an afterthought I push the litter box in with

my foot, shut the door and go back to my work. Marshall pokes his head around the corner, his expression a satisfying combination of dismay and gratitude. Sabrina turns the speaker volume up so we can't hear what now lurks behind the office door. We groove to Marshall's other favorite, The soundtrack to Hairspray. OK, but it beats Piaf on repeat.

12:00 NOON
Oh Merciful Goddess! My favorite customer plunks down $250 for my best original creation and gifts us a box of chocolate covered almonds and a bottle of Cava for later! This might keep me from sinking into a tulip induced coma.

12:16 PM
Husband stops by with Middle Eastern carry out. Not a very romantic gesture on this day, but for a man without a romantic bone in his body and a woman who is hungry, it will do nicely. There is nowhere to set anything up. All surfaces are occupied with vases of sickly sweet hyacinths and tulips and bear grass and tea leaves and pincushion protea and gerberas and callas and orchids and plastic tridents for enclosure cards and raffia and ribbons and wire cutters and loppers and pearl-top pins and bits of stems and rose leaves that smell like pesticide and paper towels and wax paper and delivery boxes and shredded paper and order sheets and pens and a couple of drops of my blood. We eat out of bags while working.

1:00 PM
Marshall sends off Hugo and Sabrina to deliver the wedding flowers, muttering something of an off-color prayer that the ranunculus bouquets hold up until 4:00 and that

46

Hugo will abstain from breaking any laws, which he is wont to do. He opens the till and passes a crisp twenty to Sabrina to make sure of the latter.

1:02 PM
Sabrina whispers to me that she hates a job where she's treated like a babysitter. If she wasn't having an existential crisis since getting married, she'd have a real job. She said this last year.

1:02 PM
I tell Sabrina she's truly invaluable, same as I did last year, then go back to begin that $250 work of art for which I get no extra twenty.

1:29 PM
We stand back, all of us, to admire my arrangement and count up the total on the stems I used. It is a luscious eruption of magentas, blues, oranges, and bright yellow-greens. I go through my bag with filthy green fingers, searching for my phone. I have to take a photo of this one. I will use it to remind myself the artist in me isn't actually dead.

1:30 PM
Back to roses. Another prick and more blood. Fuck.

2:02 PM
Trying to dissuade a customer who wants to send a box of dead sweetheart roses to his ex-wife. It takes listening to his tale of woe for me to succeed, but in the end I do.

2:19 PM
Inspired by this, Sabrina and I decide we need a breather. We gather our favorite enclosure cards together for en-

tertainment.

"I can't wait to shop in your snack aisle tonight…. Love, Petros"

(sent)

"To my little beer nut, with love, Chuckie" (sent)

"Please come back. I just got out and I need you. I'll never let you go!

Wade"

(sent with a fair amount of trepidation)

"I hope you will be a good girl when I reveal myself to you, Your Prince"

(sent, but regretting)

"To my wife, I want to wear your dress tonight, Love Pookie"

(sent, delightedly)

"These roses are dead,
  The violets aren't new,
  This is to tell you that
  I don't miss you.
No longer yours, Rod"

(declined)

"Happy VD! Your sexy lover, Norbert"

(sent)

3:05 PM

Reviewing an order in front of the cooler I feel a drip of cold water bounce off the top of my head. Effing leak. I tell Marshall to call Sammy.

3:30 PM

Sammy is explaining the problem from the top of a ladder in an English/ Romanian mash up. Marshall nods, but I know isn't listening. I stand back and admire the imaginative clusters and jewel tones of a low, English garden style arrangement I just completed for a Mr. Grabner. I even added a couple of blushing Forelle pears. A five o'clock pick up. People at the register are wowed. Marshall decides to leave it on the counter until Grabner arrives to showcase our higher aesthetic (shove the teddy bears). On the spot I get a second order to copy it. OK, no tips, but after eight hours, a little validation feels pretty good. I don't even care that the pipe has resumed a slow drip, but now over my station.

4:00 PM

The other driver, Kenneth, is back. A sprinkling of clippings from his white beard is still evident on his oily shirt, washed perhaps last week. He is following me around with a broom in his hand, annoying me with stories about younger women he asks to be Facebook friends with.

4:13 PM

Kenneth coughs copiously (an ex-smoker) and finally leaves on his next delivery route. He's just about worn my nerves through to their electrical core. When the van pulls out I feel like I've just had an inflamed appendix removed.

4:20 Just noticed it's PM

Music is off and Janet can be heard again, muffled, like a mournful attic ghost. Someone, thank you, puts on vintage Aretha and turns up the volume. Evan from LD Wholesale shows up with a couple of casket like boxes, no doubt filled with the stuff picked over this morning, but beggars can't be choosers. Happens every year—we run out of flowers and have to order more. And every year we grouse about the condition of what we get. Every year I must tighten my creative belt. But after a long stint as a human rose and tulip factory, I rather like the diversion and challenge of scarcity.

4:25 PM

Evan is kind of an ass. He won't carry the boxes up the two steps to our door unless we pay him extra. Highly suspect, but we don't have time to argue. We pay. I fashion a hat out of a basket wrapped in lavender floral foil (that dripping water was starting to make me want to divulge state secrets).

4:30 PM

Evan and Hugo are standing outside, flirting. Both of their skinny-jeaned hips equals one half the span of mine. Tempted to hurl the tortured cat into his truck while he isn't looking. Marshall has to shoot Hugo a text to get him back inside.

4:45 PM

Hugo loves my hat. He tries to make one of his own while entertaining us with the genius delivery he made on the way back from the wedding; cleverly climbing into the recipient's house through an unlocked window, as no one was home and there was no other place to leave the flowers where they wouldn't freeze. Marshall stares at Sabrina. I remind Hugo that, in his future deliveries, he doesn't need to get that inventive. In fact, it's best he doesn't. He bats his eyes and I see he's added some glitter to his lids. Sabrina sips a large latte and slinks past Marshall, thanking him for it. Marshall's hand opens for the change, but Sabrina pretends not to notice.

5:15 PM

Grabner is here and complaining loudly. Marshall explains that many customers have admired the arrangement, but the man will not have it. *I don't want this—I said to make something really great! This is to my lady—I*

5:16 PM

I stride out from the back of the store, pinch a smirk, I know what you want, I say. I grab the beautiful piece and request five minutes. At my station in back I take a tall glass cylinder, fill it with water and a few strands of bear grass, select a tall branch of burgundy cymbidium orchid, take the little Forelle pears and wire them to the thick orchid stem like testicles, shove the member into the cylinder and present it to Mr. Grabner. The loser actually loves it, gloats with pride. Gives me a tip! What a gonad. His lady must be a saint.

5:55 PM

Counting up the completed orders and what I've yet to do. Thirty-eight and eleven. My back is aching and tight. My foot is throbbing. I stretch, then take off my shoe and examine the puncture wound and wonder why I wear Crocs to work. Sabrina says it looks bad, maybe I should take it easy. She is enjoying another break, thumbing through the Feb issue of Dwell Magazine. I sigh loudly at her, then get back to the Sistine Chapel of V-Day arrangements, a $300 explosion of garden roses in a football helmet shaped vase for the wife of a pro quarterback.

6:00 PM

Kenneth returns and I'm over my ankles in cuttings. He starts to tell me about some woman he used to know in 1972 and, unceremoniously, I hand him the broom. My expression isn't friendly.

6:04 PM

Husband calls to see how I'm holding up. I tell him everything's coming up roses (funnier in my head) and I'm hoping I won't get a staph infection from the gash in my foot. Most of all, I say, I might have to break Kenneth's knee caps. He let the freaking cat out. When I do it I will use the steel end of the loppers.

6:08 PM

Marshall steps into the back to request Gottschalk's lovely forfeited arrangement. I forage to find a couple more pears to replace the ones I took, and hand it over.

6:10 PM

I hear the register. Shit yes, sold! Take that, Sexualinadequacyman! Sabrina captures and returns Janet Whiskers to her solitary confinement, but not without being ruthlessly scratched.

6:45 PM

All the last-minute losers have disembarked from their commuter trains and buses and are descending upon what's left of our flowers, lining up, on their cell phones, stupid and anxious. Marshall and Sabrina are wrapping bouquets like it's the Kentucky Derby. Her cat scratched arms look hideous and strangely stigmatic.

7:00 PM

Marshall makes the decision: we are cutting off orders for delivery. There are enough now to keep Kenneth and Hugo out until at least eight. That is, if Hugo can manage to stay out of jail and if old Kenneth, the hopeless women's Hugh Hefner, stops trying to pick up dates.

The last couple of my bouquets get looser, rather ad hoc, sillier. It's ok, the recipients are desperate Band Aid seekers, the ones who forgot. They'll take anything... as if, after eleven hours, we care anyhow. My calves are cramping and my foot is throbbing like a bloody bell. The good news is that Marshall has been too busy to wallow in the pisspool of his broken heart.

7:25 PM

An inexplicable sorrow hits me. It starts with my annual humiliating realization that no one will be sending me flowers…then, somehow, that blends together with Piaf and doomed St. Valentine, the quixotic old heart, and mixed in, just to vex me, is the helplessness of the little cat. Janet Whiskers, shatteringly irritating as she is, is only trying her best, unwittingly destined for aloneness. Under my foil hat, my eyes sting. I add a special flourish to an arrangement of scraps, the lovely peach colored dahlia I'd been saving for myself.

8:00 PM

Heavenly, dirty, empty buckets, it's over for another year! We turn the lock, sweep a lot of shit off the counters, and pop the Cava that's been chilling in the back corner of the cooler. Marshall whisks some leafy detritus from the old CD player and puts on Moby, Hotel. He disappears to check on the sequestered and forlorn Janet Whiskers. Sabrina and I sit our bones down on a couple of stools and drink bubbly out of rinsed out coffee mugs and nibble on chocolate almonds. I've forgotten about my foil basket hat. She seems to have as well. Sabrina says she wants the last track of this disc played at her funeral (she is worried about cat scratch fever). She wants modern dancers to perform and an aurora borealis light show. I say there will be legions of Teddy Bears and Mylar balloons at mine, I'll be dead and can't say no. We laugh, but we can't help thinking about death a little as we move piles of severed petals to locate the sign out pad.

8:16 PM

A hard bang at the back door. We turn. The desperate lit-
tle alarm salesman coming for revenge? Someone locked
out of the adjacent parking garage? Sabrina groans. I
take off my hat. It's only Hugo. Bustling in, keys swinging
from his pocket chain, he's hefting a cardboard box. The
box unexpectedly tilts in his hands and he almost drops
it. Edging out of his office, another bottle of wine tucked
under one arm, Marshall declares that little minx must
go under the knife and pronto. Hugo shakes his head,
batting glittery eyelashes, and reaches into the box, lift-
ing out a beefy, one-eared, scar-faced old tomcat, "Chub-
by Chester", purportedly found along his last delivery
route (we don't ask). The large orange creature emits a
wide, impatient, whining mew and spreads his toes and
resplendent claws. He may have seen better days, but he's
still got it. Hugo grins naughtily, opening the office door.
Chubby unfurls, dropping down, despite his stoutness,
like a splash of water. The door is closed. Before Marshall
can protest, Sabrina turns up the volume on Moby, mugs
are raised and we toast Love and the old sentimental saint
who pays our bills. The Cava is performing miracles on
my foot and elevating our accomplishments. We almost
forget to sign out, we are such contented martyrs.

- Christina Robertson

Lizzie Dreams of a House on the Beach

I commit to the ax
Take my vows to the hatchet
Dismantle domesticity
while dreaming of seashells
& the many ways a bone can splinter

I break eggs in the cellar,
dip my fingers in salt
to better excavate my wounds—

Rustle of a skirt
Curl of an earlobe
Hands do not understand
there is more to hold than iron and wood

Two of the same do not breed strength
they only build more walls

What can the ocean do for me?

What future is promised
for pebbles
rolled in the sand

other than the smoothing
        of rough edges?

- Ingrid Taylor

Drinking Saudade From a Bottle of Whiskey

Bring me into your awe,
your overwhelm—
This night of more
and more,

Met and left in a single moment,
this sickness for what's unseen
scratching behind a closed door.

      This drink
      uncracked
      this ice
      unsplit

How the hand curves to the shape
of a glass,
how cells return to fascia and bone
that can only stretch so far.

- Ingrid Taylor

GODDESS OF LOVE AND LIMIT

I am not here for your killing floors,
to be clean-licked and puppy-warm,
or swaddled in the numbness of lactation.
I have only a tail to pull and a body,
naked and bountiful.
I know every myth ends
with a girl in pieces,
And a mother's cry.
I am not the salve
you expected, milky-white
And orbed.

This is my gift: in the weight of your blood
And the stone of your heart
I burst
slick and screaming as a newborn,
fists clenched on light and air.

I am overfed on sacrifice, flooded
with toxic grains and grasses.
I have cut off my horns
and crawled inside your membranes,

Chosen many small deaths over one.

- Ingrid Taylor

THE MALL PARKING LOT

The summer is wasting away. I am wasting away in this room. Nothing to do, nowhere to go. I should just drive. The room smells like old coffee and cinnamon. I leave my cave. Dad is sitting in front of the computer, feet propped up. Mom pushes her glasses against her nose, reading. Bailey is working in a law office, making money. The house is still and tired. I finger the phone in my pocket, waiting, always waiting for something to wake me up. I have a little calendar running in my head: Three days till band practice and two days till *His* show at The Landing. Although I haven't seen him for a month, we've been talking every day and I've learned a lot about him. I like that he's older than me. He seems independent with a job and college.

I walk out into the backyard. The smell is blue, tropical and imposing. Florida has the best skies in June. Mom planted hibiscus flowers around the above-ground pool. She spends a lot of time in the pool listening to talk radio. I wish I could forget about all this trouble and just float in a pool forever. I must...I do...like him. Not in that floral bursting way but in a way. The smell of jasmine punches my gut. I walk back inside with dirt on my feet, tracking it on the floor like the dogs.

"What's up?" Dad tilts his head forward and looks through the mirror behind the computer.

"Oh, nothing, I think I'm gonna go to the mall. Real quick."

"Okay, have fun."

Did he have a knowing twinkle in his eyes?

The mall parking lot is vacant and sad. I remember being here with some friends last year. It was the first time we hung out. We biked the trail and our bikes almost got stolen. I was funny that day. Really funny.

The moon is a scar on the skin of today. She rises beyond the parking lot and away from the consumers driving back to broken homes with more stuff they don't need. Society has never been a good headspace for me. I hate this force-fed postmodern mentality. It makes me sick, sick I tell you—I tell me, I guess. I'm gonna scream right here and they'll have to call the police, and I don't care.

The tone. My chest constricts. I flip open my phone and read: "Are you coming to the show tomorrow? I really want to see you."
Thrill upon thrill.
My fingers feel out the words. "Yes! I can't wait...to see you."
Check mate.

I bounce over a brick road, taking the route I've google-mapped but never driven. I see it, his house. I drive by slowly. The lights are on inside. He's so close. My hand leaves the wheel and stretches toward the windshield, toward the brick house and the light in the bedroom window. Tomorrow is a step nearer.

- Kathleen McGuire

Two White Russians

Fifteen minutes after we took off the aircraft levelled, and the red seatbelt sign went out with a soft "bong." Immediately a fat man at the front of the plane stood up to rummage in the overhead locker. The captain's voice came painfully loudly over the scratchy intercom to tell us – first in Russian, then in heavily-accented English read from a laminated card – that we were at four thousand meters above Minsk on the way to our cruising altitude of seven thousand meters, that he intended to fly the aircraft to Warsaw, and that he hoped we were comfortable. I was stuck in an aisle seat down the back, just in front of the toilets, with a woman holding a sulky-faced baby across from me, and didn't feel at all comfortable. I consoled myself that it was only a two-hour flight.

It had been nearly dark as we walked across the wet tarmac to board the plane, with red, green and white lights shining fuzzily around us in the damp grey air. But up here above the clouds the sun was still setting, big and flaming like a smelting furnace. It sat low above the horizon, level with us, and sent bright orange-pink rays spearing through all the cabin windows. The flight attendant got up from her fold-down seat, smoothed her navy-blue skirt, and walked slowly along the aisle. As she passed through each of the horizontal bars of sunlight she was, from shoulders to hips, painted fluorescent pink; she seemed not to notice.

Somewhere down below us stood the bare concrete polyhedrons of Minsk airport, and half an hour back from there by bus the city of Minsk itself, with its grandiose Stalinist boulevards, its deep underground metro stations, its football stadium ringed with socialist-realist sculptures, and its groves of white birch trees. And also down below, in the pale-green kitchen of a small flat in a five-storey apartment building on Gagarin Street, boiling water on the gas stove for coffee, lighting a slim white cigarette, opening a bottle of Armenian cognac, generally going about her business, was Mila.

Whenever I thought of Mila I saw her mop of brittle, frizzy dyed blonde hair. That was in one way unfair, because Mila spoke at least three languages and had an extensive knowledge of art, music and Russian Orthodox iconography. But she had chosen to define herself by this harshly artificial blonde hair, with its perpetual black roots, so she could hardly blame anyone for thinking of it first when she came to mind.

I was very fond of Mila. In fact, she was the main reason I came to Minsk as often as I did. My employers, the UN Media Assessment Office, believed I was in Minsk to monitor levels of press freedom in Belarus, White Russia as it used to be known. In truth, to report honestly on the level of press freedom in Belarus in those days was a simple task; there wasn't any. End of report. But I could always drum up sufficient degrees of grey about the subject to keep the paper-shufflers in head office interested in sending me back there.

What Mila was doing in Belarus was another story again. She was originally from St Petersburg, and if you accepted her account she had been by turns a junior badminton champion, a concert pianist and an art historian. She had married at least twice, the last time to a White Russian. Coincident with the Soviet Union disintegrating more or less overnight, this husband had disappeared, leaving her with Belorussian citizenship, a flat in Minsk, a grand piano, and not much else. Since then she had made the best of a bad job by working as a Minsk tour guide, looking out, it was probably not unfair to say, for her next husband amongst the occasional Western tourists she guided.

Other than UN bureaucrats and nervous, tight-lipped Belorussian government officials in cheap shiny suits, the only two people I knew in Minsk, indeed in the whole of White Russia, were Mila and a man she introduced to me as her cousin, Kyril Demianovich Shustov. Although it was impossible not to like the fellow, I wasn't certain his given name was really Kyril, I actively doubted his surname was Shustov, a well-known Soviet brand of cognac, and I didn't at all believe he was Mila's cousin. A big man whose twinkling eyes were almost hidden by round apple-red cheeks, and with thin brown hair receding from a forehead bulging with intelligence, Kyril was a brilliant chess player, a one-time USSR junior champion, or so Mila told me. He had gone to seed from alcohol, and now, instead of the tense, silent atmosphere of international chess competitions, he was to be found every evening in the park in front of the Trinity cathedral, cracking jokes while playing six games at a time for drinks.

He and Mila had travelled together through India and Nepal, he told me, pulling out a tiger's tooth he wore on a leather thong round his neck. When he was sober or, better, half-drunk, he was a vastly entertaining conversationalist in either Russian or French, and quite funny even in English. We three had a number of enjoyable evenings drinking vodka or cognac well into the night in the little kitchen of Mila's Khrushchev-era flat, telling jokes, topping each other's stories and generally laughing a great deal.

People drank at home then; it was not so easy to drink at night in public in Minsk. The only place I knew was the downstairs bar in the Hotel Minsk, its booths tricked out in beige velour and populated with a number of big men in ill-fitting casual clothes, sitting long over a single glass of beer and looking over the few foreign guests with a flat stare. It wasn't an atmosphere conducive to relaxation. Much better to drink at home, or at the home of your friends, or at the home of your friends' neighbors.

I craned forward in my seat to look out the airplane window. The sun had finally set, even from up here, and the sky was blue-black. All I could see, as I peered round my fellow-passenger's shoulder, was my face reflected in the window glass; unshaven, strained, looking older than I liked to imagine myself.

I was wearing the same jeans and jacket I had on when I arrived in Minsk nearly a week before, and I felt scruffy and shabby, a man who deserved to be seated at the back of the plane. It wasn't actually my fault; the airline had contrived to lose my baggage between Vienna and Minsk. They said 'mishandled,' scrupulously avoiding the word 'lost,' but in six days my bag hadn't turned up, and I suspected I wouldn't see it again. At first I'd resisted buying new things in case it jinxed the chance of my luggage being returned, but in the end I'd had to get a shirt and socks and underwear. You can replace all the stuff in that bag, I told myself, and you should be above fretting over mere possessions. But when I remembered that the 1950's Russian Pobeda watch I'd bought in the Karlsplatz flea-market a fortnight ago was among those possessions, I wasn't able to achieve quite such a Zen state of mind about my missing bag. Perhaps I should have shaved today, I reflected, to push my appearance a bit closer toward respectability.

The hostesses were distributing tea and coffee, starting at the front of the cabin. It would be a while before they pushed the trolley down to the back, and by the time it did their patience and quite possibly the coffee would have been exhausted. I leaned back in my seat and closed my eyes.

I had to face facts; I could not continue with this half-relationship with Mila. I had met her two years ago, on my first visit to Minsk. She had been sent by the tourist office to give me a day tour of the city. We had hit it off straight away, so it seemed to me, and over the next ten days we ate and drank together, we went to the flea markets and the ballet together, in due course we slept together, we even went to church together. Now whenever I went to Minsk, I cancelled the hotel reservation the office made for me, stayed with Mila, and used my expense allowance to buy her presents in the airport duty-free shops, Italian shoes and jewelry and good cognac. Up to now that arrangement had suited us both, but I could see it wouldn't last much longer. Mila wanted a husband, not a fly-in fly-out lover. After my last experience of marriage, I didn't want to be anyone's husband, and certainly, if I were to be completely honest, not Mila's. Nevertheless, she had alluded to the subject of marriage several times during this last visit, and I could not continue to ignore it. In fact, I had to admit that Mila's fondness for me was probably conditional on the prospect that I might one day be her husband. If I told her outright that was out of the question, I could not be sure her affection would maintain its present level.

Last night we had gone out to dinner at a restaurant that still bore clear marks of its Soviet heritage; big white sheets tied over the chairs, rolled-up apricot-colored napkins standing in the wine glasses, a large number of waiters whose eye it was impossible to catch, a menu which boasted a wide selection of dishes that weren't actually to be had. On the other hand, when the food did arrive, there was a mountain of it; marinated fish and cutlets and pelmeni, potatoes and chicken wings and vinaigrette and red caviar and salo, and there was sticky-sweet

Moldavian brandy and beer and chilled, triple-distilled Moskovskaya vodka. The place was full, with a constant swell of conversation and laughter.

Toward ten o'clock a fellow set up a small electric piano and a girl emerged with a remarkably short, tight spangled dress and a microphone. A purple spotlight was turned on them, and together they turned out a seamless sequence of sentimental Soviet-era songs. People got up and danced while others clapped and sang along. It had been fun. We had got home half-drunk, and eventually gone to sleep tangled up together in Mila's narrow bed.

But today had been different. Today had been twelve hours too long for Mila, it was obvious. She had been edgy and uncommunicative, and she had jumped nervously every time her phone rang. I knew what that meant. Another friend of hers was coming to Minsk, arriving the same day I was leaving. She didn't want to offend me, but neither did she want to offend the newcomer; one never knew which might turn out your best card in the end.

I had no right to expect anything better, of course. I had made no promises to Mila and asked for none, and she owed me no particular loyalty. But on the evidence of her reaction to today's overlapping visits, it was clear I either had to make some permanent arrangement with Mila – even if not take her up strictly on her suggestions of marriage – or accept being more or less a customer, which was an unpleasant way to think of myself and of Mila; or worse, lose her altogether.

I understood that part of Mila's desire for a husband was to get away from Minsk for good, and if at all possible to gain European citizenship, exactly which sort not being of critical importance. That was understandable. But however I was to arrange myself with Mila, I could hardly take her back to Warsaw, because, leaving aside questions of visas and the like, there I already had a girlfriend, Agnieszka. I was comfortable with Agnieszka and the routine of our life in Warsaw, which was where my work was, and which in any event is twenty times a better and easier city to live than Minsk.

If I didn't find Mila so extraordinarily attractive, it would have been very easy, but unfortunately I did. She had really got under my skin. Perhaps – on a generous view – five years older than Agnieszka, Mila was clever, abrasive, sexy and clever again by turns. She had a huge store of knowledge in subjects that interested me, a desert-dry sense of humor, and boundless energy, provided she didn't have to get up before ten in the morning and had a full supply of cigarettes and coffee. Her slightly weathered beauty was highly attractive in what I liked to think of as a decadent way. If I had to make a final choice, it was not quite so simple.

I opened my eyes. The second hostess was coming past with bottles of water. She was plump, but it suited her. When she smiled, even in the distant looking-just-past-your-shoulder way that airline hostesses smile, she showed a charming dimple in each cheek. Maybe I should forget about Mila and Agnieszka and make a concerted effort to woo this Belavia air hostess. Maybe she lives in the unknown suburbs of Minsk, or maybe even in a small town outside the capital; we could have a lovely romance, walk through the quiet streets at evening, eat at the local inn, lie warm and smooth and urgent together under a feather coverlet in her bedroom. And maybe I ought to have drunk two fewer glasses of vodka in the departure lounge, if I was going to indulge myself in such absurd fantasies.

The red-faced baby across the aisle was showing unmistakable signs of being irritated, throwing its head from side to side and kicking its legs. Inevitably it would soon start screaming, and there was still over an hour of the flight to go.

I really couldn't see how I could formalize my relationship with Mila. I didn't know anything about her except what she'd chosen to tell me, and even I had realized that much of that was at best an approximation of the truth. But then again, did that really matter? Did I need an historically accurate account of a woman's life to decide whether I wanted to live with her or not? And come to that, had I given her a completely candid account of myself?

And then there was Kyril. He'd never got in the way between me and Mila, but if I was going to look at this business clear-eyed, it was sufficiently obvious he was Mila's lover when it suited them both. Of course, he could not offer Mila an EU passport, so there would be no question of them getting married, but in making any plan concerning Mila, I had to remember that Kyril was at least on the fringe of things.

The woman across the aisle was fussing a plastic baby bottle out of her bag. Just possibly, the infant might be persuaded not to cry, at least for a little while longer.

The baby must have remained silent, and I must have dozed, because the next thing I knew was the sound of the captain clearing his throat over the loudspeaker. We were beginning our descent into Warsaw, he told us, and the flight attendants should prepare for landing. A honey-colored voice that I suspected belonged to the plump hostess then supplanted the captain's, telling us the usual things about trays, upright seat backs and washrooms. I didn't feel properly awake until I was clambering down the steps to the tarmac, with a chilly Warsaw wind driving fine, stinging rain into my face.

Over the next couple of weeks I was pretty busy in the office, and beyond that I was taken up with being back in Warsaw and seeing Agnieszka. We went to the opera, and to hear Rafal Gorzycki's band play at Tygmont. We had dinner with our friends Piotr and Anna, we went shopping, and in general I had no chance to think properly about Mila or what I should do.

Then on a clear chilly Monday morning, three weeks after I'd flown out of Minsk, I received a phone call in my office. It was Kyril. I'd never given him any of my phone numbers, but I'd given Mila this office number; of course she knew what it meant that I hadn't given her my mobile number.

Anyway, Kyril didn't beat about the bush. He had rung, he said, to tell me Mila was getting married in April, to a German, and she had a favor to ask me; could I lend her a thousand euros? I told Kyril I didn't have a thousand euros to lend anybody, but I would give Mila 500 euros as a wedding present, which I would send to her at the Western Union office on Lenin Street. Where was the wedding? In Berlin, Kyril said, she's getting a tourist visa so she can get married in Berlin, and then, if all goes well, an EU partner visa. All this news tumbled over my head very quickly, like a big wave. I told Kyril I would send Mila the Western Union receipt number, and asked him to pass on my congratulations on her marriage.

Only after I hung up did I wonder why Mila hadn't rung me herself. Perhaps she felt embarrassed? No, that was hardly the Mila I knew. Then I thought of all sorts of things, things I wouldn't have had to think of if Mila had rung me in person. Perhaps she was indeed getting married, but Kyril had called on his own initiative about the money. I mean, I liked Kyril, but things are hard in Belarus, and you couldn't be surprised if a man decided to try his luck, if he knew the friendship would shortly end anyway. Or maybe Mila wasn't getting married at all, but had asked Kyril to tell me she was, to see how I'd react. Quite quickly, I persuaded myself I had to ring Mila to find out.

It took me some time to get through. It was not easy ringing a Belarus mobile number from outside, even from a UN office phone. But in the end she answered; there was a second or two delay on the line, making our conversation even more disjointed and difficult than it would anyway have been. Yes, she was getting married. And going, she hoped, to live in Berlin. 'Amongst Germans,' she said, "unhappy people who make everyone around them unhappy." I had resolved before I rang that, if it turned out she really was getting married, I would not under any circumstances ask Mila why, but at this I forgot my resolution.

"Well why, then? If you feel that way, is it worth it, just to get the residency visa, or citizenship, or whatever you'll get?"

"Not just for the visa, Martin. Not just the visa. I am alone here, and I know you are not going to marry me. A woman on her own, it's not great. And Martin, I am not so young any more." I heard her drawing on a cigarette. I could imagine her very clearly just then, standing in her kitchen, leaning one hip against the plastic-topped table, her frizzy blonde hair haloed in the light from the window, holding the phone in one hand, and one of her thin menthol cigarettes between two arched-back fingers of the other.

In that moment I felt terribly sad for Mila, and even, for a moment, sorry for myself, although I knew what she'd done was entirely reasonable. It was true, I was not going to marry her, or otherwise rescue her from Minsk. Expensive presents and good times are all very well, but not enough to sustain a whole life. And I had to admit I'd known that all along. So our conversation, our last conversation, ended with me wishing her all the best;

it felt limp, but what else could I say?

After I hung up I realized I'd forgotten to mention the money. Just as well, I supposed. I could hardly ask her if it was true she'd put Kyril up to hitting me for a loan. I'll send her the money anyway, I decided; I owe her, at the very least, a decent wedding gift.

I had absolutely no right to feel hurt that Mila was getting married, none at all. But already I felt her absence keenly, now I knew I wouldn't see her again. Memories of our days and nights together in Minsk rushed through my head, and those memories seemed unbearably sweet. I reminded myself that I couldn't have expected Mila to go along the way we were for ever, and that I was lucky to have the time we had. And I told myself it was good I didn't have to tap-dance round the increasingly pressing issue of marriage with Mila any more, nor disappoint her any further by refusing. And, yes, I had lost Mila, but what did I still have in my life? A good job, a pleasant apartment near the Old Town in Warsaw – a city I loved – and a nice girlfriend. All a man could ask for, really. Belavia Airlines had even returned my missing luggage.

So I went about my life. But I was left with an undiminishing feeling of absence, of loss. I tried to put Mila and Minsk out of my mind, from a belated sense of loyalty to Agnieszka and my life here, or that's how I explained it to myself; in truth, it was to stop myself feeling bereft and disconsolate.

One night a few weeks after all this, I took Agnieszka to one of the new cocktail bars that had recently sprung up in Kazimierz. A well set up little place, with a long bar, quiet jazz, and discreet, soft lighting. I found us a table and went up to order our drinks. The handsome young barman wore a waistcoat and bow tie.

"What will you have?" he asked me.

"Give me a couple of White Russians," I said. It

was meant to be funny, a private joke with myself, but just for a second there, I felt as much like crying as laughing.

- Peter Newell

His eyes were dark with shame when he said, "Please let me swim out to sea."

As if our story could end here, in a nondescript Mexican hotel somewhere on the edge of the Sonoran Desert. It had startled me when he opened his hand and showed me the box of pills, the blue ones and white ones, the small sleeping pills. "I already took a handful," he said.

The mind races to keep up with the heart. The heart flowers open despite the wreckage. This was no honeymoon in Mexico. This was the edge.

"We could do it together," he whispered. I longed to curl up in his lap and sob. Instead, I told him to give me the pills. He shook his head, weary, at the end of his rope, someone I barely recognized. Me, a widow and a grieving mother; he with the loss of his mother, his work, his home, his reputation.

"You can't do this to me," I told him. "Give me the pills. I can't go through it again. "

Both my partner and my youngest son had died from suicide. My partner was bipolar and his suicide something he had warned me was coming. My son's death three years later was a shock. It completely derailed my life. I could not endure another loss.

I tried to grab the pills. He was stronger and kept me locked in his grip with one hand, tears in his eyes. He shook his head. "I want you to help me. I want you to lie down beside me and caress me and let me swim out to sea. I'm probably crazy just like my mom," he whispered.

I felt sick. Hadn't I heard all this before? I crawled closer, straddling his leg on the rough, thin bedspread.

"No, I will not let you go. You cannot do this to

me."

No, Alejandro, I do not release you. I am your destiny. You are my husband and this moment is my redemption. I refuse to be a widow again.

Finally, the tequila, the pills, the nights without sleep followed by eight hours of driving took over his body.

"Give me the pills," I said. Our eyes locked.

"I'll just put them under the pillow," he mumbled, and we laid down, tightly wrapped around each other.

We were married only on paper. We had made a choice and taken a risk and tonight, that choice and that risk bound us as tightly as true marriage vows ever could. I tried to stay awake, but my body gave in to deep exhaustion.

We slept, dreamless, breathing together, alive.

When we awoke the sun was shining and we were hungry. We couldn't drive the car into Mexico—Alejandro had forgotten the car registration, so we parked the car with a gas station attendant and took a bus. Our first priority was to get something to eat. Alejandro asked for directions to a seafood restaurant and we caught a taxi. I was happy to hear Spanish all around me. Spicy condiments were lined up on the table and the women were dressed in elegant clothes. Alejandro had managed to track down the name of the hotel where his boyfriend Felipe had stayed. I wanted to kick back at the table and order another michelada, but he escorted me out the door as soon as we finished eating.

At the hotel, he convinced the receptionist to give him the list of phone numbers that Felipe had called from his room. I was astonished. In the United States, this would have required a search warrant but here, his charming, persuasive smile was enough.

Next, we had to get a local cell phone. We spent hours at the cell phone company, seated in hard plastic chairs, while he admired the women, dressed in more revealing outfits than women stateside, and I laughed and asked him if he was sure he was gay. When we finally emerged into the bright heat with a phone, he dialed the numbers the receptionist had given him and established that Felipe was still in Hermosillo, presumably with the paintings that he had taken across the border.

A dispute between himself and a gallery, over who would represent an artist he had represented in the past, had escalated out of control. When he finally was able to reach Felipe, Alejandro insisted that the paintings taken across the border had to be shipped back and he would pay for it, that Felipe owed him at least this much. Hopefully, this would put the problem to rest, the alarm that had led to his fear that immigration would deport him and ruin his chances of returning.

"What shall we do, Gretel?" He always used his pet name for me when he felt loving, in control.

"Since we are in Mexico, let's go to the beach. Bahia Kino isn't that far away. There must be a bus there."

Alejandro was not interested in public transportation. He decided that we should buy a vehicle. We spent the afternoon at the used car lot, negotiating through the complications involved in selling a car to someone with a United States driver's license. The car dealer agreed to let us take several vehicles for a test drive, but the one Alejandro was determined to have was the shiniest and boldest—a brand new red pickup truck. And he had enough cash to pay for it. The car dealer was willing to drive Alejandro to the license bureau, make copies of the title and paperwork, and let him take the truck for the weekend.

We needed beach gear, so we stopped at a Walmart.

I didn't know whether to be amused or shocked that my shopping excursion in Mexico was at a Walmart instead of the *mercados* I loved with their hand-made clothing. Alejandro came out in shorts, flip flops, and sunglasses. I found a flowing pink skirt, a pink bolero sweater that fit over my white camisole, and sandals.

Hermosillo was hot and dusty, and the sun glittered on the highway. This turned to gravel as Alejandro zipped along, despite the jolts and bumps. As soon as we arrived in Bahia Kino, the tension in my spine melted with the sound of waves hitting the shoreline and the smell of fish and sea.

Bahia Kino is a small town that hugs the curve of the bay across from Baja California, so the water is clear, gentle, and warm. The town of about 7000 inhabitants is laid back with little to do but laze on the sand (gringo side) or fish (Mexican side.)

We stopped at a restaurant with a thatched palm roof open to the breeze. It was fairly empty in early evening and we sipped micheladas in relative quiet. While we waited for our orders of fish tacos, I had an impulse to take off my sandals and walk through the warm sand to the the rippling wavelets. I waded out further, tucking my pink skirt inside its elastic. The sun was just starting to set, glossing the bay in crimson and gold. I breathed in sea and breathed out peace.

Later we walked the beach, laughing and holding onto each other, tipsy with *micheladas* and relief. Felipe had been located, Alejandro was not locked up in jail or deported, and that the future was a blank slate.

I witnessed a transformation in Alejandro. He was relaxed and happy in a way I had never seen before. He loved the sea and the lazy swing of the hammock, speaking Spanish and being the man with the cash while the waiters catered to his whims. Suntanned, he was more

handsome than ever, his dark eyes sparkling, his shoul-
ders thrown back, the man I had fallen in love with, not
the anxious bully nor the pretentious art dealer. It felt as
though a façade had melted away. Although it broke my
heart to head back to my life in the states, I trusted that
he would land back on his feet. His *joie de vivre* was back.
The next morning at the internet café, I made a plane res-
ervation for the next day.

Tears filled my eyes as we said good-bye. As the bus
pulled out of the station, he mouthed *"Ciao, princepesa,"*
quoting from the movie, "Life Is Beautiful."
        Did he know at that point that I would be coming
back?Or did he only think of the next day, making sure
the paintings were shipped off, clearing his name, look-
ing for work, deciding whether to stay in Hermosillo or
move on, arguing with Felipe as they fought for control
of the relationship?

Alejandro eventually landed in Puerto Vallarta, a city
with a thriving arts market. He and Felipe soon opened
a small gallery and made enough during their first high
season to survive through the winter—then they broke
up again.
        The practicalities of how I could quit my job and
fly down to Mexico eluded me until one day I noticed a
flyer for the Spanish school *El Instituto Cultural* in Oaxa-
ca. I would go to Puerto Vallarta to teach when my class
finished. My old life was peeling away, layer by layer.

I boarded the plane scared, determined, and wondering
if I was taking too big a risk.
        Alejandro picked me up at the airport, his shirt
soaked and sweat dripping down his forehead. "Did you
run here?" I asked in surprise as he welcomed me with a

kiss.

When we got outside to the parking lot, I understood. The tropical heat of Puerto Vallarta was oppressive, humidity at 100% and climbing. I had dressed in jeans for the plane ride and immediately sweat collected between my thighs. We stopped for lunch at a seafood restaurant, Alejandro driving down cobblestone streets with a flourish.

The apartment was up three narrow staircases with two iron doors to unlock. I didn't know what to expect but he opened the door to a lovely spacious apartment.

I changed into a cotton skirt I had bought in Oaxaca and Alejandro offered me a beer. The refrigerator held a dozen *cervesas*, a bottle of tequila, a jar of olives, a bag of limes, coffee, and a jar of jam. On the counter was a bag of *pan dulces* he had bought for breakfast. Behind the kitchen counter were shelves with pasta, rice, crackers, and more cans of olives.

"I guess we have to go shopping," he said, rubbing his chin as he looked at the empty shelves of the fridge. I couldn't wait to fill up a basket with *tomates, pepinos, cebollas, chilis, agucates, papayas, platanos, y mangos,* and buy fresh *tortillas* from the *tortillería.*

After our beers, he suggested that we take a walk to the beach, crossing the swinging suspension bridge over the Rio Cuale, the bridge swaying with each step.

During the plane ride, the only thing I could think about was whether I was making the right choice. *Show me a sign*, I prayed. Although I wanted to be with Alejandro more than anything, I didn't trust him, didn't trust the moods, the volatility, the way he could hurt my feelings.

But I was in his territory now. His country, his language, his culture. In the gay scene of Puerto Vallarta I would be an outsider. The only thing I had in Mexico was the narrow thread between us of our intertwined histories of loss and grief.

I wanted a fresh start. I wanted to fill my senses with color and aroma and tastes, to be somewhere where death is a part of the cycle of life and I wouldn't feel so strange. Here I would be connected to the one person who demanded that I "get over it."

As we stood overlooking the bay, I noticed how good he looked. His dark features glowed with vitality and we were giddy to see each other, but mostly he was happy to be by the sea. We were watching the sun sink and trail its golden flare across the vivid aquamarine of the bay when a storm cloud began to fill up the sky behind the mountains. In a split second, it blew directly over us. Hard drops fell. By the time we spun around, the sky opened up in a torrential deluge and we were instantly soaked.

Clasping hands, we shrieked as we ran through the puddles back to the apartment. We slipped and skidded over the bridge and then once we got home, removed everything to hang up on the clothesline. I pinned up my skirt, peaches-and-cream lace camisole, white cotton shawl, peach bra and undies next to Alejandro's beige shorts, blue boxers, and green T-shirt, making our own rainbow. He looked out at the line and chortled, "What will the neighbors think? They know I am gay!" and we doubled-over in laughter.

"*¡Que escandalo!*" we chimed in accord.
We sat on the balcony, amazed at how quickly the river had overflowed its banks after one storm. Later that night, the boys would come out to fish, their pants rolled up, casting nets over the rushing waters.

I remembered how years before, during an *Earthwalks* expedition to Chaco Canyon, the Native American women had told us that rain was a blessing.

"We have been blessed," I toasted, and we clinked glasses. I felt flooded with an irrational happiness. *The first storm of the rainy season,* I mused, as he made white wine spritzers and handed me one. *This was the sign I was waiting for.* It seemed to be a yes.

-**Wendy Brown-Baez**

Down to the Caves

Ricky is little, so his don't-mess-with-me look doesn't work too well. He moves around fast like a cricket. And his lunchbox doesn't help—he made it out of plywood and it's padlocked. It has a picture of Bach on one side, drawn with a wood burning iron. Kids in the lunch room always look when he opens it. Last time I glanced in it held his secret hand-written sheet music, a pair of home-made brass knuckles, and a can of those grape leaf things filled with mushy rice.

Behind our combined middle school and high school is a creek bottom where kids smoke. Ricky and Scott and Mike and I have been going there forever to shoot our b-b guns and dig caves in the mud banks. Once a year the carnival sets up in a pasture on the other side. We like to camp out when it's there so we can listen to the far-away sounds of people being let down and hoisted up again on rides.

That's what we did a couple of weekends ago. Scott got a twig fire going because it's part of his wanting to live off the land. His big dream is to survive a wilderness plane crash that kills everybody else except him and a girl who doesn't like him much at first, but then comes around once he fights off bears and brings her wild salad greens. He stayed mad at me for a week once when I told him that "wolves mate for life" doesn't mean they have to have sex or they will die.

So Scott was stirring his coffee can stew with a stick when Julie Dimmit, out of our league in the tenth grade, appeared without a sound like a ninja girl. Suddenly she was just there, sitting on a high bank edge. She asked what we were up to without really seeming to care. We were looking around, gearing up to say something impressive, when she pulled a big bottle of vodka out of her backpack and took a drink. She glanced at the cave we'd been working on. Took another hit. Then she held the bottle out to Mike who, like a dumbass, looked at us before he took it. I don't think she noticed, though, because she was looking up into the big trees on the creek's far side. I remember exactly what she said. "Looks like you would want to build a treehouse instead of digging holes. Then you could see that neon on the carnival rides lighting things up. All those sad colors twirling around." Scott laughed and Julie looked at him like an owl spotting a mouse. She snatched her bottle back from Mike, who had been kind of making like he was taking sips from it. But after a while she smiled. She stood up and dusted off. It was getting dark but the last light was catching her. She looked amazing. Then she said, "I like being way up high with nothing on. I'll do it with the first one of you boys who builds a decent treehouse over there." She slipped her bottle into her backpack and was gone, with the four of us blinking up like her outline was still visible.

We went over things and decided she had to be just jacking with us. But Ricky was real quiet the whole time. And because his contractor father always has lots of scrap material laying around, Ricky's the one who single-handedly went to work and got a treehouse built in one skip-day.

It had a railing all around, and a canvas tarp roof. When the rest of us showed up, Ricky looked like he might not let us up. But after a minute of staring, he threw a rope ladder down. What a view I said when we climbed up. Ricky said it wasn't furnished yet. But he already had a cot mattress set right in the middle of the platform. For some reason none of us much wanted to look at it. Then Ricky said he needed our help with the hardest part, which was, well, letting Julie in on developments. We sure would have rather helped with the hoisting and nailing.

It turns out Julie's father lost his job for real quick reasons and they all moved away in one night right after she made the offer. Ricky went into a slump. But after a couple of days we were back to digging on our caves. Sometimes Ricky would look over at the tree house. Finally he said we should have a party in it at least once before the carnival closed, so we could see the lights.

We met there at dusk last Saturday. Scott brought corn chips and bean dip, and I brought the pink champagne I had stolen from my sister's car the day after her prom night. Ricky brought his telescope. We all looked through it, watching the hair of screaming girls fly back when the Tilt-a-Whirl whipped around. Ricky said it looked like sea creatures he saw once in a tide pool by the ocean. I said I bet Julie would have really liked the view, and Ricky's nod was him thanking me for saying that. We watched until men started dropping the tents in moonlight.

Thunder and lightning drifted in then, big clouds moving our way. So we got our stuff and went over to our caves. Ricky said he'd be along in a minute. It was starting to rain when he came running in. And he must have used a whole can of gas, because across the way the treehouse blazed like a Viking ship funeral.

Soon water was rushing past our entrance and it was time to leave. We covered our heads with old pizza boxes and ran, hollering all the way. Splashing out of the wildest place we knew.

-Daryl Scroggins

LAMENTATION

Your body said, 'Take, eat,' but you were no messiah.
You were Dionysus, you were Don Juan, you were Valentino.
I was entertaining at best, then extraneous
when your wife called you home.

Every week was Holy Week:
Thursdays my feet washed with your mouth,
Fridays dark movie houses and strangers,
Saturdays quiet and throbbing and desperate.

We were buried in the tomb of shame,
but every afternoon came a resurrection
after the breaking, the entering.
I rose again and again.

-Denise Alden

Punished

She gives you very specific instructions. Do not divert, your wife said. It's your fifth anniversary, and this year, she gets to make the rules. The plan: You are to meet her in the hotel lobby bar under the chandelier to the far end at 8:00PM, sharp. She'll be waiting for you there. You are to wear your fanciest slacks—pressed and lint-free—with those Armani leather loafers she'd bought you last anniversary. Remember? She likes you in a white button-down dress shirt—no tie—open at the collar so she can see your bone. Shirt is to be tucked. Do not forget the belt, Remi. You choose the black one, leather. Then, you are to take a cab from your home in Highland Park all the way downtown—Michigan Avenue—to the Drake. Your cab's waiting in your driveway—just beyond the white picket fence—while you deadbolt the front door. There's enough food in the bowl to last for Kitty. Do not drive, she warned. You will not be coming home tonight.

Downtown, off the street, you're through the revolving door with snow on the tips of your loafers and the scent of ice in the lake air on your skin. Somehow, you're reminded of clean sheets when the crisp of your chill hits the warm leather lobby. You take the scarf from around your neck. Undo your coat to drape over your arm. Wipe your feet while eyeing the room for her, nervous enough to feel the need to look busy. She said she'd be waiting for you. You check your watch. 8:10.

Where's the bar? you ask the front desk attendant. You think you recognize reservation in the demure woman's face—as if she knows something about you that you don't—when she turns her gaze toward her computer and points down the hall. You shift your scarf from one arm to the other. Thank you, you say, moving your head to catch her line of sight. She grins, redder in the cheeks than when you'd arrived.

Enjoy your stay, she says, eyes down.

Right, you say, wondering about her assumption that you were staying the night.

Toward the bar, the hallway is carpeted in plush maroon. Along the wall, framed photos—lake landscapes in black-and-white and candid street shots of Chicago city-goers. One woman behind the glass catches your eye because the angle is from behind. You wonder how you can feel so much without being able to see her face.

With the bar just ahead, you walk slowly—with trepidation—shifting your coat from one arm to the other, your heart in a race to get to her, to make certain she's here. Plus, you're late, and she was very particular about you being on time for this date. Sharp, she'd said. Remember? Shit. Stalling, you run your fingers through your hair, smoothing down the back. These unknowns make your clothes feel tight. You unbutton one more at your collar, wave your hand at your face for air. Your wedding ring. She'd told you to remove it. Right. You struggle with the platinum band, hands swollen from unease. Finally, it's off, in the palm of your hand, then slid down the slim front pocket of your slacks. Suddenly, you imagine the young busty front desk attendant. You turn to look behind you, over your shoulder, toward her post. The hallway seems narrower down there. You shake your head with a fleeting thought about being late enough so your wife doesn't wait—what the young woman might agree to with you and your naked ring finger. Your scarf drops. Bending down, you notice the stains on your shoes—sleet and sidewalk salt. With the scarf's tassels, you wipe your loafers clean before continuing on.

There she is. Right where she said she'd be. Bar. Far end. Under the chandelier. You recognize your wife only by her long red hair gathered at her front. When you approach, she's twirling the bundle, combing the ends with her fingers. Then, she spreads the hair evenly along her front, her whole chest draped in a thick curly blaze. Her tight black dress has a lace collar held around her throat by a small button in the back. There's a slit down the back of the dress from her nape to her waist. A strip of her skin shows—like milk spilling down the length of her spine. You can't remember the last time you saw her in black. The wife you know loves color. When she shifts her slim body in the high-backed bar chair to lean into her elbows on the bar, her naked shoulder blades cradle the curve of her long backbone. You want to touch her. To run your finger over the small bone at the base of her neck, a pearl cushioned by the rippled shell of her clavicle. You know these unseen parts of her as only a husband would. Your mouth waters.

She's laughing lightly with the bartender when you slide into the seat next to her. There's an empty cocktail glass between her hands on the bar. She prods the bottom of the glass with her straw, flips her hair, then tucks a strand behind her ear. The bartender asks her if she wants another—Another Manhattan, Miss? he says, and she only grins, gazing at him. Then, with her fingers, she digs out the maraschino on its stem from the ice at the bottom of her glass. She tilts her head back under the dangling cherry, then drops the piece into her mouth and looks ahead.

Sorry I'm late, you say, situating your coat to drape over the back of the chair. Then, you reach over to touch her shoulder. When she leans away from you, your fingers are left to tremble, suspended like a fly to her nectar. I get it, you say. You're mad. I'm late.

Do I know you from somewhere? she asks you.

Very funny, honey. Look, there was traffic on the toll road, and then the cab …

She swivels the chair to face you, uncrossing her bare legs. When she leans toward you, you're reminded of the first time you inhaled Chanel Number 5 off her neck years back. The scent of your wife's skin taught you how to recognize the knockoff. The kind you'd come to find lingering on your coat the day after your one and only indiscretion involving another woman from the office. You knew right away, it was not the real thing. The cheap one clung to your clothes, up your nose for days. Your wife's Chanel would blossom around her only when she was actually present in the room. Like when she'd lick her fingers and wave her wrist to turn the page of the New Yorker while across from you during breakfast in the nook against suburbs through bay windows. When the table was cleared and your wife was gone, there was never a trace of her to be found. Suddenly, you wonder about that one other woman and the knockoff—your infidelity. For an instant, you consider how things would be different if your wife had found you out.

Now, here, her scent—like a landmark—is your only reference point. Looking at her, you feel as if you're roaming an unknown city—down dark alleyways of her bare legs under thigh-high spiked heel boots; aside the architecture of her whole lean body under the fit of her dress. This woman is no sculpture you've seen before. How she's painted her face—blood-red lips and thick lines—makes you yearn for her, so you gather her whole face in your gaze. When you look into the shards of her blue eyes like glass, you're reminded of a weapon. You reach your hand toward the open space between her knees. She shuts her legs.

Honey? she says. Quite the presumption, calling me that on first sight.

Right, you laugh, we're playing now.

Is something funny? she asks.

Alright, darling, you say, but you're nervous, and you know she sees it. This foreign woman still knows you in ways only a wife would—like how your body moves when you're pretending. You smooth your hair back with both hands. Let's go to our room so I can properly wish you a happy anniversary, you whisper toward her.

I was married, once, she says. Not tonight.

Come on now, honey. What do you want me to say? She slaps you then. One terse rap on the back of your hand, against the knuckles. You look at her ring finger. Naked. Suddenly, you feel compelled to play along, as if you have no other choice. Okay, okay, you say. What happened?

He was a very bad boy. You stare at her—brow furrowed; mouth tight—as she continues. I think all men need to be punished, she says. She opens her legs wider. You sense her nakedness when she puts one hand to each of your kneecaps and digs her fingernails in. You lean back as she leans forward. She's close enough for you to smell the sour cherry of her cocktail on her tongue when she says, Do you want to get punished, Sir? You watch her mouth, the way she uses all of her parts when she speaks. How her mouth cloaks the stress of the word with a slipknot of motive—punished—how she pinches her pink tongue between white picket fence teeth—punished—the way she folds the word along her gums— punished—her lips, skin tight around the shape of those sounds—punished—a word decapitated by her perfect mouth at the end. A clean cut. She grins, and suddenly, you're throbbing.

Well? she says.

Yes, you say, yes I do, darling. I do.

Tonight, you will call me Mistress. She takes a key card out from her purse, sets it on the bar. Do you understand?

Yes … Mistress.

Room 1010. Wait exactly thirty minutes. Knock three times to be let in. She runs her hand through your hair. That scent of Chanel off her wrist unravels you. She twists your ear, pulls your head back, and says, Do you understand me?

Before you can answer, she's gone.

Tenth floor. You slide your hands down your pockets roaming the hallway to find the correct room. 1010. You check your watch. Right on time. Sweat from your palms is hot against your thighs through the fabric of your pressed slacks. At the door to the room, you stop. The top floor view will show you the lake, once you can manage to get yourself inside. You gaze down the hallway. There's an exit route—stairs to the roof—just up ahead beyond the room. Suddenly, you're desperate for more air, for city wind, for ice against your skin. You imagine the openness up there, how you'd step to the edge and look over. With shallow breath, you tug at your shirt, venting near the armpits, then untuck it from your beltline. Black leather. You'd remembered. Then, you draw a long breath in through your nostrils. You retain the breath—at the top of your lungs—as if it was your last. One. Knock. Beat. Your heart. Beat. Echo. Empty. Cavity. Your chest. Two. Knock. Beat. Exhale. Knock. BeatBeatBeat.

When your wife opens the door, your chin has dropped to your chest. You lift your head, slowly, gazing along the length of her, starting at her feet. Spiked heel boots have not been removed. One spike holds her weight while the other props the door. Long legs are bare, fair against black leather. Her sheen reminds you of snakeskin. She has removed her black dress from earlier. Black lace garters are fastened around the top of each thigh. Tiny bows on each belt excite you, and your arousal by bits of innocence feels like sin. Suddenly, your forehead is hot, your cheeks are hot, the nape of your neck—hot—your whole face burns. Attached to the garters—one wide strap of black. It runs across her sex and up her torso. At her ribs, the strap splits to cover each breast—situated over her nipples—but you can see the round of pigment you know so well, the skin that spreads beyond the strap's width, skin the color only a lover could describe—her whole chest unfettered, yet hidden. Then, your gaze inches along the length of her breastbone—her long ivory torso like a tusk—your mouth wet imagining the bareness hidden from you. Your slacks begin to constrict, as if your sex takes a breath of its own.

What is this? you say, and you're shifting from one foot to the other, trying to see behind her into the room. She situates her body to block your view—arms, chest stretched across the doorframe. Suddenly, you're angry. You try to dodge her. She does not move an inch. What is this? Her body—close enough to breathe her in—quells your exertion like a hydrant. Her power matures with the Chanel under latex on her skin. Move aside, you say, but you're meeker now, afraid to make contact with her eyes. What is this? Your body's hardening is uncontrollable. Its reaction—like a spasm—confuses you. You feel like the hunted with a hunger that gets you trapped. You do not want to like this.

Let me in, you say toward the floor, and you hear yourself whine like a frustrated child.

No talking, she says, spikes planted.

Just let me through, you say.

You will not speak unless spoken to.

Alright. Just let me in.

You will call me Mistress.

Let me in.

Do you understand?

Let me in, Mistress.

Look at me.

I can't.

You will.

I won't.

When she draws her arm out from behind her back, you clasp your hands behind you as if cuffed. You—hunch, rounding into yourself. She—broadens, more bullish than before. There's a leather riding crop in her hand. She runs the whip up your leg, along your inner thigh, to your hard middle. She continues. Slow, slow, slow, she crawls the keeper upward, along each buttonhole of your collared shirt. Just under your chin—SMACK—she stops, then forces your gaze toward her eyes. Your face is lifted like meat on a spatula. Your hands are kept clamped down on one another right where they are—behind you.

You will, she says.

The mask is a band of black. Her perfect lips—stained in red—are fuller in the absence of her wide eyes. You've always adored her wide blue eyes. Now, through the slits, she glares—blue eyes sharpened into little knives. Her long red hair is braided, resting along her front like a whip. You look beyond her toward the view. On the lake—white winter light, like ice. White light on glass—ice. You shudder. She stands back—just slightly—away from you. The entire anonymous woman.

You take a full look. Her most private parts edited like words on the page of her body—slashed but legible—and in that last moment before you enter the room, it occurs to you just how fine the line really is. One line of latex—a flimsy belt—the only bar between the intimate and the exposed. Is this enough to keep you out of her? No one else is here to stop all this, to stop you from devouring her with desire as your authority. Your distress can't stop this. If you lunge at her, would she stop this? (You're desperate to stop this.) You close your eyes. Stop this, you say, imagining your modest wife—floral prints at the kitchen sink, dish soap on her hands. Open eyes—a nameless Mistress. Your abdomen aches for her.

May I enter, Mistress? you say, and you don't recognize your own deep voice—weaker and restrained. All control is lost. Your appetite for her—your curiosity—moves you across the threshold. Afflicted.

DO NOT DISTURB. She deadbolts the door.

Stand there, she points to the edge of the bed. Do not move.

This room has high ceilings. The bed is king, made perfectly with white down, white pillows. When she walks toward the windows, you notice how her strap is flossed around her backside. She draws the heavy blinds. White light is thickened by the dark. You feel heavy on your feet when she turns toward you to approach. Carefully, she lays her whip on the bed. Then, she moves behind you, reaching around to your front. She runs her hands down your chest, unbuttoning along the way.

Wait, you say. Let me look at you, Mistress.

No talking, she says, then pinches the tender skin around your nipple. She removes your shirt. She runs her hands along your front toward your groin. You squeeze your legs, afraid her touch will ruin you completely. Her hands are cupped around you when she breathes into your ear. Then, she turns you around, to face her. Unbuckles your black leather belt, zipper, boxers. Step out, she says, and you know she means from your remaining clothes. She unthreads the belt from your slacks. Naked, you shiver—eyes on the windows wishing for that icy view—your hands covering yourself. She kicks your clothes to the side.

Yes, Mistress.

Bed, she says. Facedown.

Yes, Mistress.

You recognize your belt lashed against your backside by its smell of leather over your own scent. Whipped by your own belonging, you squirm, angry. What the fuck?

Now, now, she says, and spanks you again.

Stop this.

Turn over.

Stop it right now, you say, but you don't try to get up. Instead, you do as you're told. You flip over shyly, trying to cover your parts with a pillow, as if she's never seen your body before.

You're on your back now, and there she is, above you. Propped by your elbows—your sex like a saber—all you want is to take her. She unties the strap at her neck. You watch while the lines across her body are erased. She holds the strap taut between her two fists. Then, she comes to you, climbs on top, her knees to either side of your hips. You bring your hands toward her ribs, to try to touch her, but she wedges each wrist under a knee—her weight, the only restraint. It's enough. You lie back. Somehow, her power is enough. Enough to constrain you. She leans forward, her full bare chest aimed at your face. She lifts one knee to remove your limb from under her, then takes your hand, guides your arm above your head. You suck your stomach in when she fastens one wrist to the frame of the bed. Now, the other arm—bound. Then, you're widened—chest spread along the width of the bed—and you look at your own body, gazing side-to-side, following the breadth of your chest, along the muscles of your arms spanned like wings, and you think … you think, somehow, you feel beautiful like this. When you look at her then, you grin, softly, softer than you can ever remember. She shifts her head, sits back on you. She breathes. You shift your middle up toward her, your intent—to be inside her. But she rears. She's on both knees. She situates the black strap over your eyes. So tight—too tight—she ties. It's time, she says, and in the darkness of your mind—on the cross—you are no longer beautiful. You're blind.

A knock. You hear your Mistress walk to the door. Who's here? you say, and you cross your legs trying to hide yourself. Who is that? you say with invisible aim, Is someone else here? Silence. The whip against your thigh. No talking.

The other woman comes to you. You smell her youth when she's close—a harmless scent of sweet cherries and lime. She touches you. Cool skin from the air outside. You feel her on the bed. She spreads herself on top of you. What? you say, No, no, get off of me, you say, and you shift your bottom half. Where is she? Where's my wife? you say, but the other woman has you pinned. When she rubs herself along your front, you feel the prime of her tight chest, this woman, this younger woman's scent, the sweetness of her breath—you're dying for her … you're dying for her to STOP—she licks you from groin to throat.

You've slipped inside her.
She tightens.
You crack.
She flexes.
You moan.
She shifts.
You shatter.
You're coming.
You can't hold your body together.
I'M GOING TO EXPLODE! you yell, and you think of your wife—the real thing—simple and floral, and you're crying, you're crying now when you say, Please, I

don't want to come. I don't want to come, you say. Please! You thrash your head from side-to-side. You hate them— this other woman and your Mistress. The blindfold has come down slightly from one of your eyes. You're still inside her, and you're yelling, Please don't make me come! but she's moving faster now, so you bite your bottom lip. You try to catch a glimpse of the other woman. You do. The front desk attendant rides you like a bull. No. You bite yourself harder. Blood. Iron. You hate yourself with a raging fire—for your infidelity now, for every indiscretion of the past. Punished.

Finally, you hear her. It's your wife's voice—your Mistress—from somewhere across the room. Next time you find your way to another woman, she says, I will say how. I will say who. I will say when. Do you understand?

Yes, Mistress, you say, while the attendant kisses your mouth.

Go on then, she says to the front desk attendant.

Yes, you moan, yes, yes.

Finish him.

Finished.

In the morning, she's left you a note. You are to meet her in the hotel café for coffee and a nice scone. Don't be late, honey! Your wife is nowhere to be found. Thick blinds are now pulled back. Yellow light off the lake warms you through the glass. Defeated, you run your finger across the window. Ice makes water out there, on the sill, in the sun.

Downstairs, you look for her in the café. There she is. Far table, near the windows facing Michigan Avenue. She doesn't see you when you look her over from a distance. Her hair is pulled back into a tight bun. The collar of her floral blouse is high-necked, covering her entire chest. Her shirt is tucked into jeans, and on her feet—simple sneakers, white with laces. She's got a scarf around her shoulders, and she sets her spoon down perfectly after stirring sugar into her coffee. You take a long breath and straighten before you approach.

Morning, you say.

Morning, she replies, face sheltered by her menu. She shifts her glasses on her face. I'm thinking Eggs Benedict, she says, eyes down.

Yes, you say. Great. Good. Thanks, by the way.

For what? she asks.

The scone.

Right.

Great.

Good.

You slide down in your seat, bring the menu up in front of you. Over its edge, you're sneaking glances at her. Her eyes are plain now—magnified by her glasses—natural and wide like a trusting child. Suddenly, she moves her eyes toward you. Quickly, you look down. Then back up. But her eyes are down again, and neither of you seem able. Eggs Benedict? you ask, staring at your lap.

Right, she says.

Great.

Good.

When the waiter comes to take your order, your wife gives hers while you look beyond the café to the lobby. At the front desk, there she is—the other woman—now in uniform as you'd seen her just yesterday. A sharp breath up your nose and you hold, moving your menu up to cover your line of sight so your wife can't see you look. Immediately, you ache. You look at your wife, still ordering. Then back again, at the other woman. The attendant catches your glance just as you're about to look away again. She grins. Shakes her head, looks down again.

Remi, your wife nudges your leg with her foot under the table. Speak, she says.

Speak?

Your order.

Yes … dear.

Right.

Great.

Good.

-Emily Tobias

SAUDADE

My sister insisted we stay up till midnight to celebrate my twenty-first birthday. I'd forgotten about this long-ago incident until recently, when I celebrated another milestone birthday.

In the living room of our childhood home in Kirkwood, Missouri late that summer night, Janet was sprawled across a blue loveseat. I sat across from her at the Steinway Grand, silently stroking the keys to avoid waking our sleeping parents. Both of us were petite, different timestamps of the same person: long, dark brown hair and brown eyes, lounging in matching pastel cotton pajamas.

Waiting, counting down, we talked and laughed and reminisced, mostly about summertime activities we'd shared during our childhood. We talked about visiting our grandparents in Bronxville, New York each year. About sandy days at Long Island's Jones Beach, drinking Nehi Orange soda and eating deviled ham sandwiches our grandmother prepared. About going to the New York World's Fair in 1964 and hearing Dave Brubeck play "Take Five." About going to Daddy Michael's for ice cream in White Plains, New York. About singing "Gary, Indiana" at the top of our voices on our long car rides to New York, about using a comb and tissue paper to create makeshift kazoos for the trip.

We talked about summer evenings back in Kirkwood: collecting lightning bugs in jars, playing "Mother-May-I" on the back sidewalk, or tag with neighborhood kids. About going to the swimming club with our mother, eating hamburgers and french fries for lunch, topping it off with a frozen Zero candy bar. About Janet copying me by wearing a nose plug when she swam. Despite being five years younger, she remembered nearly as much from those years as I did.

We reminisced about my efforts to entertain her by making shadow puppets on the wall when she was only four. We shared a room then, and I used light cast from our night light as the backdrop for my show. Teaching her to spell short words those same sleepless nights: cat, dog, mom, dad. Both of us lying in our twin beds with white, chenille bedspreads, careful not to let our parents hear us giggling and talking past our bedtime.

I told her how crazy it was, staying up instead of going to bed. Waiting for a birthday. "What difference do a few hours make?" I asked her, half seriously, half in jest. "We won't miss anything if we wait till tomorrow morning to celebrate!" But she was adamant we greet my twenty-first birthday together, at midnight, and so our reminiscing continued.

* * *

That birthday is now a distant memory, along with my little sister, who died suddenly nearly ten years ago. When I search for the word that best describes the loss I feel, what comes to mind is a Portuguese word: *saudade.*

A lifelong student of languages, I'm obsessed with the meaning of words, how untranslatable many are. But people like to simplify life and, to that end, they strive to simplify language. It's as though they visualize words on a vast spread sheet. In Column A is a word in one language. Column B is next to it with its exact meaning in a second language. The same thing in Column C, and so on. In theory, more than 6,000-mile-high columns representing every word in every language rise up to the sky, graphed mathematically, logically…. erroneously. Thankfully, the world is more complex than that.

Dictionaries translate *saudade* as "longing." That's partly accurate, but it doesn't capture the depth and physicality of the word. So, not a bull's eye, but maybe it hits the circle *next* to the bull's eye. *Saudade* is deeper and wider than "longing," the difference between being nicked with a pocketknife and stabbed with a dagger.

Saudade is a pendulum. One minute it swings back to the past, transporting you to memories of times together, staying up till midnight to reminisce and celebrate a birthday, for instance. Then it swings forward to a future without your loved one, those rips in the fabric of the universe where your lives will no longer intersect: birthdays, trips, family gatherings.

"What difference do a few years make?" you may ask yourself.

Quite a lot, as it turns out.

- Linda Murphy Marshall

RABBIT FUR

She was French—and her upright posture, blonde hair, long flowered skirts and soft white and grey rabbit fur jacket added up to perfection.

I wanted an identical fur but when I said this to her, she laughed a bit and said I looked lovely in my own clothes. I had excellent taste. She told me her jacket would not change my life.

I know it wasn't an expensive jacket. I was sure it smelled of her skin, possibly the perfume she wore: tea rose. I didn't speak of it frequently, didn't repeat how much I admired that jacket, how much I wanted the exact same one. After all, I was an adult, a young married woman with two children. My husband was a stern father and this raised many problems. I had a responsible job.

Before our sessions, I often went to Dresdner's, a restaurant a few blocks away from her office on the Upper East Side and I ordered bacon, lettuce and tomato sandwiches and iced coffee. One day my therapist walked in with two teenagers. She rarely spoke of her family but on one occasion she had mentioned that she had grandchildren who lived and went to school in the neighborhood. She was wearing her rabbit fur jacket. They held hands, the three of them.

"I can't believe it," the girl said in a loud voice. Then the three of them began to laugh.

I felt like an orphan. When they left, my therapist nodded at me as they passed my table. I felt left out and helpless.

At our session an hour later, I demanded to know why she hadn't introduced me. Wouldn't it have been the polite thing to do? Was I a non-person? I thought of dinner parties where my husband regaled company with stories while I sat silently by his side.

She understood. She explained that to enfold me into her family in even a casual way might raise unrealistic expectations that I would become part of it. I had my own family. And her family was not as ideal as I might imagine.

The following week, I entered her waiting room early. I was often early when I drove in from the suburbs to the city. I had to look for a parking space in her congested neighborhood.

If I got one right away, I either went to Dresner's or headed to her office. She shared the office with another therapist so the front door was always unlocked. I enjoyed sitting in the waiting room staring into space and thinking.

One Wednesday, she and I entered the waiting room at the same time. She was wearing a navy blue cashmere jacket. Large silver buttons cascaded down the front.

As we walked into her office, I said I missed seeing her in the rabbit fur jacket. What happened? She had given it to the maid, she said.

I sat in my usual chair and clutched the arms. Why the maid, I thought. Why hadn't she given it to me? I felt I was going to cry but swallowed back my anger and oncoming flood of grief.

"Are you alright?" she asked.

I could not get myself to look in her direction.

"It was old," she said. "It would mean more to you than was appropriate." Perhaps I would try to become someone I was not, but we needed to talk about it…talk about how much it meant to me.

I could not tell her—it meant love and fashion; meant the tenderness she'd always shown me. Could not tell her if she disappeared, I would always have that jack-

102

et. I would wear it every day inhaling her confidence and her beauty. Could not explain that it stood for the life I wanted to live.

That day and the following days, I yearned for the jacket. I wanted to buy it from the maid. The maid, I thought, would be glad to have the money.

One night I dreamt I stole it, that I had broken into her apartment, scattered all the clothes in the closets on the floor in a huge pile and finally found and grabbed that jacket. But just as I was about to put it on, it burst into flames.

She died eight years ago. I still think of her walking into the office in that jacket, a red and black silk scarf draped around her neck and oh, her long flowered skirts. I can hear her voice, the French accent, the way she softly explained why I couldn't have what I yearned for and that one day she hoped I would value my own choices. Even now, I sometimes wonder where the jacket is. Perhaps it's at the bottom of someone's closet or completely discarded.

But I shall never forget during that first season with her, never forget the scent of it and the way she flung it quickly in such a casual way over the back of her chair. Flung it on the chair as if it were an ordinary garment, some piece of clothing anyone could wear.

- Joan Halperin

Fields was slipping around with Red's woman, the woman we called The Other Red. Everyone but Red knew, but that morning it looked like Red knew, too. He arrived at the factory, alone in his red pick-up, stepped out of his truck, naked to the waist, wrapped a red handkerchief around his head, and drew a large circle on the asphalt with a piece of red chalk. As a fiery sun rose behind the maple trees bordering the parking lot, he sent me inside to fetch Fields. A little before starting time, the other men sat out front waiting for the work horn to sound. No one tried talking anyone out of anything. No one asked silly questions. The men drank their coffee, smoked, and watched from under their baseball caps.

Most mornings, The Other Red chauffeured Red to work in the shiny red 'Vette he'd bought her to drive. The men would wink at one another as she slid out of the driver's side, her long, lean legs flashing like knives. They grinned when she walked around the car to the passenger's side, her buttocks rolling inside a short, denim skirt. There, she leaned into Red as he leaned back against the 'Vette's front fender. For several long minutes, the two lovers pawed the ground and kissed like teenagers, although they were forty if they were a day. The men called her a looker and said she'd been around and would leave Red the minute someone better came along. I attributed such talk to envy and lust because the men also said Red would kill you if he found you with The Other Red.

Maybe, that's what attracted Fields.

Already at his work station because he liked an early start, he laid down his tools the moment I told him Red was calling him out. No doubt, he'd been expecting this or something like it. I followed behind as he strode through the factory, stripping his shirt along the way.

When he entered the chalk circle, he lowered his head and charged. Red side-stepped, raised his fists, and took a stance. Fields recovered and charged again, this time tackling Red and forcing him onto his back. Red blocked a right and caught Fields flush in the face with his own right.

Working at Voyager RV was my job that summer of 1973. Recently graduated from high school, I planned to attend a down state university come fall and needed to earn as much as I could. The better-paying line jobs went to full-grown white men, so I worked for minimum wage on the set-up and clean-up crew with Juan, a Mexican from Guanajuato, another white kid who insisted his name was Slick, and an older black gentleman who answered to Sweep. Except for Red, who called me Kid, the other men, Fields included, called me Shithead or College, as in, "Hey, Shithead, you missed that piece of scrap over there," or "Hey, College, bring me another box of nails."

Red, tall and rugged as a hickory tree, was an ex-Marine sergeant who'd served in Korea and Vietnam. I kept him well-stocked with two-by-fours and two-by-sixes and took special care to keep his work space clean and neat. Using a collection of clever jigs he'd designed, he built every roof for every RV that passed down the line. He worked alone, refusing to share his piece-work pay with another man because, the men said, he needed every penny to keep The Other Red in style. That was probably true, but on those days when the heat in the factory topped one hundred degrees and the vending machines ran out of beverages, Red grudgingly slipped me a few dollars under the table to help with roof assembly.

I also ran set-up for Fields who built bathroom and kitchen cabinets alongside Schumacher, a soft-spoken Amish man. Twenty years younger than Red and The

Other Red but marked by a scarred face and bad disposition, Fields was also a Vietnam war vet, a sniper with one hundred certified kills to his name. Once, while I was taking a leak, he stepped up to the urinal next to mine. He finished his business, then for what appeared to be no good reason, slammed the urinal's handle with such force and hostility it broke. He ignored my presence and left me wondering if I should report the vandalism, a firing offense, to management. On reflection, I decided to pretend nothing had happened, and if it had, to act as if I knew nothing of it.

Back on their feet, Red and Fields fought, grunting and sweating, jabbing and slamming. A few of the men cheered. Some placed bets one way or the other. No one tried to stop the fighting or call for management to step in. Fields was strong and bullish. Red, although older, was quicker and more agile. Fields, anyone could see, was a brawler, capable of landing and absorbing heavy blows, whereas Red was a boxer, calculating and accurate.

That summer, I was in love, or thought I was in love, with a girl who faced a final year of high school. She wore my class ring around her neck, and until recently, we'd planned to maintain our relationship when I went down state. We'd planned for her to join me there the following year. But, now, our plans were in limbo due to something stupid I'd done. In fact, it looked like I might lose my girl altogether. Kat had engaged in what turned out to be an innocent flirtation with a stranger, a guy a couple of years older than me who attended our local community college. Misreading the situation, I'd felt betrayed, and white hot with jealousy, I'd sought to even the score by dating another girl. It was only one date, and nothing happened, but in a small town, word got around. Now, the stranger posed a real threat.

Red said the stranger wanted only one thing, and Kat would see through him soon enough. He said if things were meant to be between us, she'd eventually come around. Fields, though, said I needed to forget Kat. According to Fields, once I was down state, I'd have all the college girls I could handle and would never think of Kat again.

One moment, Red pressed his advantage. The next, Fields held the upper hand. He landed bone-crunching body blows loud as thunder claps. Red's punches snapped like lightning, lacerating flesh. At one point, they separated, breathing heavy and glaring at each other from across the chalk circle. Fields shouted that just so Red knew, it was The Other Red who'd come on to him, not the other way around. Besides, Fields said, she was too old for him, and he was tired of her. He grinned and said he was in the market for fresher meat. Red hollered he didn't give a damn about any of that; he was there for one reason only, to administer a beating Fields would never forget. Then he made his way across the circle and popped Fields in his right eye with a dynamite left.

The factory foreman, Frankie the Hammer, came outside, pushed through the crowd, and asked how long they'd been at it. One of two brothers from Tennessee who worked in Sidewall said maybe ten minutes. Frankie said if this didn't wrap up by the time the work horn sounded, he'd, by God, put an end to it himself.

They called him The Hammer because he had fists like hammers and also because his weapon of choice, should he require one, was a ballpeen hammer. In addition to serving as Voyager RV's foreman, Frankie moonlighted as houseman for the factory owner's illegal gambling operation, sports betting and card games, ran out of the backroom of an uptown restaurant. Everyone knew the police looked the other way so long as they got a piece of the action and Frankie maintained order.

Something I missed since Kat dumped me was hanging out at her house. I missed playing catch with her little brother and munching on the chocolate chip cookies her mom used to bake when I came to visit. Chocolate chip, she said, because they were my favorite. I also missed how her dad called me Champ. Back in the spring, I'd made it to the state finals in the 880 and mile, earning a slot as a walk-on down state and a shot at a scholarship if I made the team. You've got this Champ, Kat's dad would say, and when he did, I felt like I did have it.

As for my own parents, things weren't going so well. My mom had moved out of the house, saying she could no longer live with my dad. I didn't know why she felt that way or what it would take to bring her back. All I knew, she was gone, staying at a toll road motel and refusing to come home. In her absence, my dad had become sullen and brooding. He'd switched from beer to whisky.

After exchanging a series of blows, Red and Fields separated, breathing hard. Both men bled from the mouth and both had slowed. They circled, each looking for an opening. Red no longer jabbed and feinted. Fields no longer taunted and clowned. But neither man showed any sign of backing down, and for the first time since they'd started fighting, I wondered what would become of The Other Red.

Something else I missed since our break-up was making out with Kat on her sofa after her parents and little brother went to bed. It wasn't like we were having full sex—

Kat wanted to save that for marriage or at least until she was engaged—but we were fooling around, kissing and touching in places I'd never touched or been touched. Red said if Kat was the right girl for me, it was worth waiting for. Fields said he wasn't surprised I'd lost Kat to the stranger. He'd advised all along that unless I insisted and put it to her, she'd find someone who would. Now that she'd left me for the stranger, Fields had no doubt he was putting it to her all the time.

I guess you'd say my mom was a looker, too. She managed a women's clothing store and liked showing off her looks in expensive clothes and shoes. She was also smart enough to get what she wanted, and what she wanted was a woman's clothing store of her own. My mom believed that the man who owned the store she managed was plenty wealthy enough to seed her start-up; all he needed was a little persuading. My dad, a salesman, prided himself on being able to sell anything to anyone. The summer I worked at the RV factory, he sold cars, but he'd sold real estate, building supplies, and life insurance before that. He liked to say the best sale he'd ever made was selling himself to my mom.

In the end, both eyes swollen shut, his face a moonscape of cuts and slashes, Fields couldn't rise from his hands and knees. Blood, thick as motor oil, oozed from his nose and dripped from his chin. Red, clutching his ribcage and swaying, stood over him. Someone called an ambulance just before the work horn sounded. When it did, the men turned away, speaking in hushed voices and heading inside. Frankie the Hammer made his way into the chalk circle and announced to Red and Fields that he had no choice but fire them both for fighting on premises. It wasn't up to him, but that was the rule, and he meant to enforce it.

A few minutes later, an ambulance arrived and took Fields away on a stretcher. Red washed up in the bathroom before walking unsteadily to his pick-up. I walked alongside and asked if he needed anything, and he said he reckoned not. I asked what this meant for him and The Other Red, and he said he reckoned that was up to her. "I chose her out of all the women in the world," he said, "Now, she needs to choose me, or not. She's a full-grown woman and can do as she pleases."

I said I was sorry he'd been fired, and he said make no mistake, he'd been fired from better.

After Red drove off, Frankie the Hammer took me aside. We were in peak season for RV production, and with Red gone, he needed a new roofer, pronto. Because I was the only man who understood Red's jigs, I was the logical choice to replace him.

I appreciated The Hammer's vote of confidence but reminded him I was headed down state in a couple of weeks. "After that, you'll need another new roofer. Doesn't it make more sense to put that man in place, now?"

Frankie shook his head and said he needed a roofer today and believed I was the best man for the job. "Look," he added, "it's none of my business, but you'll be making a big mistake by heading down state. The odds of your down state shot working out are about as good as drawing to an inside straight. You'd crazy to throw away a good-paying job for odds like that. Besides, you stay in town, you'll be in a better position to win back your girl."

"I don't know if I can win her back."

"You'll never know if you don't try."

I gave Frankie the point and told him if he thought I was man enough to fill Red's shoes, I'd do my best, at least for the present. "As for my giving up my down state shot," I said, "I need to think on that."

Frankie assured me I'd have plenty of time to think while I was building roofs, and I'd better get on it. Not long after, the police arrived asking who was responsible for the ass kicking Fields had received. I told them I'd been late for work but heard that a skid of sheet metal had fallen on him. Juan claimed to have been in the bathroom, Frankie the Hammer in his office, and neither Juan nor Frankie admitted to seeing anything. Slick said he'd been in Receiving accepting a shipment of window air conditioners. Sweep muttered something about not knowing anyone named Fields, and Schumacher pretended to be hard of hearing.

That evening, after assembling twenty roofs and paying Juan a little under the table to help me lift the last few onto the sidewalls, I swung by Kat's house. Although covered in sawdust and sweat, I had something to say that needed saying in person. Kat's mom answered the door, welcoming me and going on about how nice it was to see me again. When I asked to speak to Kat, she replied that, unfortunately, her daughter wasn't home and, lately, it was hard to know when she would be home. "Is there a message I can pass along?" she asked.

I didn't have to be told who Kat was with or what they were likely doing, but I did have a message. "Let her know I stopped by. Tell her there's some things we need to talk about."

Kat's mom gave me a sad smile. "I'll do that. I'll let her know. Are you doing all right, young man?"

"Yes, ma'am. Thanks for asking."

When I turned to walk away, she called out, "You take care, now."

Before I reached my car, Kat's dad pulled up, home from his job as a supermarket manager. "Hey, Champ," he said. "How goes it?"

I replied I'd been promoted to Voyager RV's roofer and was thinking about staying in town come fall.

"What about your shot down state?"

"It's a pretty long shot."

Kat's dad frowned. "Maybe," he said, "your chances are better than you think. Anyway, chances like that don't come around every day."

"I was hoping if I stayed in town, I'd see more of Kat."

Kat's dad put his hands on his hips and stared at the ground. "Well, I hope that works out."

"I mean, if she hasn't made a final decision."

Kat's dad said he doubted she'd made a final decision, but this wasn't a decision he could make for her.

After that, we shook hands, and he wished me the best, down state shot or not.

When I arrived home, my dad was on the screen porch, relaxing in the pink light of a fading summer's day and tuning in the Cubs game on WGN radio out of Chicago. If there was anything he loved more than having my mom on his arm, it was baseball. Before they'd married, he played minor league ball but never got his shot at The Bigs due to a shoulder injury. Now, he followed and cheered the Cubs, drinking CC and Seven while listening to their games.

When asked how my day had gone, I described the big fight. My dad said it sounded like a real humdinger, like Ali versus Smokin' Joe. Then I told him about my promotion to Voyager RV's roofer. This was a man's job, I explained, one that had a future and paid good money.

My dad finished one drink and poured another, 7-Up fizzing on his ice. "What about your shot? That won't wait."

"I know, but it's a long shot, like drawing to an inside straight. Besides, I can take community college classes at night and save enough to go down state in a couple of years, scholarship or not."

My dad nodded. "Well, working for a while and saving a little money isn't such a bad idea."

"Anyway, if I stay around town, I'll be able to see Kat."

"I thought she was seeing someone else."

"I don't think she's made her final decision."

My dad chewed ice from his drink. "I hope that works out. It's hard to know with women."

That prompted me to ask how things were going between him and my mom.

He shrugged and sank a little deeper into his chair. They'd talked earlier in the day, he said, but he didn't know if he'd made headway, or not.

"What's it going to take for her to come home?"

"You know," he said, "if you were to stay here this fall, instead of going down state, she'd be more likely to come home."

"You think so?"

"I'm not saying what you should or shouldn't do. It's your decision, not mine. But it would make it easier for me to close that sale."

I said I needed to sleep on it, and he agreed that was a good idea. He added that he just wanted me to know what was at stake.

I left my dad to his Cubs' game and went inside. Exhausted from a long day's work, I cleaned up, ate a micro-waved dinner, and called it an early night. But the sleep I'd hoped for refused to come.

I couldn't help thinking about Kat in the stranger's arms and tried to understand how it was possible that the special feelings she'd once claimed for me could now be felt for another. I thought of my mom lying in a motel bed, toll road trucks rumbling past, their bright lights shining through thin curtains. I wondered how she slept at night and who she thought about before sleep arrived.

The next morning, I slid out of bed, my nerves jangly as a set of keys on a ring. Although numb with fatigue, I knew there was only one way to clear my head. I pulled on my shorts and running shoes and slipped past where my dad snored, out cold on the screen porch, an empty bottle of Canadian Club at his feet.

We lived on a country road with working farms and a few houses set farther apart than in a suburb. Large maple trees lined both sides of the road, their leaves hanging heavy in the late summer heat and humidity. Fog blanketed the farmers' cornfields, and roosters crowed, rousing their hens. It took a while, but eventually I found a familiar rhythm, my legs strong, my feet light on the pavement.

I ran past barns and fences and the old high school with its new football stadium. Three miles in, I needed to turn around. I needed to shower and dress for my new job, but I was breathing easy, sweat flying, arms pumping. So, instead of turning around, I continued to run, the one thing I'd done better than most since I was a little boy, allowing my feet to make decisions my heart and mind couldn't.

I didn't know what other compromises Red had made in his life that would allow him to settle for The Other Red after she'd been with the likes of Fields. But the farther I ran, the clearer it became that even if I won Kat back from the stranger, she'd never again be the Kat I'd loved.

I didn't know what shot Kat's dad might have passed up or how differently my dad might have turned out if he'd gotten his shot. But the farther I ran, the more my feet said I had to take my shot however long it might be.

And I didn't know what it would take for my mom and dad to get back together. But the farther I ran, the more I realized it wasn't on me to make that happen. No one wanted to be in Frankie the Hammer's cross hairs, and eventually I'd have to explain myself to him. But that morning, I let my feet do the talking. I followed my feet into the rising red sun, feeling it, really feeling it. Feeling like I could run all day.

- Gary Powell

WORD

Maybe
were I devoted enough to father a dictionary
as he necessarily was and ultimately did
undertaking a long and tedious task
affixing loyal nouns to straying definitions
tailoring the parts of English speech
to the intercourse of American tongues
keeping my infinitives from splitting
my participles from dangling
distinguishing shades eyelashes apart
among denotative and connotative expressions
which we must utter as sentient, verbal beings—
maybe then I could believe it—
(alleged, anecdotal, possibly apocryphal,
given the babble over time of a rumor mill)
a scandal in the lexicographer's personal life
and an exchange that occurred with his wife
when she discovered him in the arms
of a mistress behind a door ajar, and exclaimed,
Well, Mr. Webster, I am surprised.
No, he is said to have corrected her, it is we
who are surprised; you, my dear,
are astonished.

- Ronald Deane Watson

The Lenten Affair

Two wild roses are having a fling
in my back yard. From an early spring
and throughout a lengthy summer,
they lay low, drank deeply, took root
and won their small victory. Lately,
daylight wanes to gray-scale afternoons.
Jet-stream air descends from someplace
north of Saskatchewan, as dry leaves
rattle on winter trees, and yellow petals
wither like old men. Most blossoms
would have sense enough
against such odds
to quit. But despite drought, lost light,
and the clicking tongues of alarm,
these darlings thrive.

- Ronald Deane Watson

Don David

On the morning of October 31 – exactly one and thirteen days since teaching Borges's "Pierre Menard, Author of the Quixote" and exactly one and thirteen years since reading *Don Quixote* himself – David woke up and had a thought: that Don Quixote and Sancho Panza were, in fact, the same person.

He wasn't immediately perturbed. Everyone knew that, on some level, characters in novels were just aspects of their authors. That wasn't the issue. What bothered him was the idea that *two* could be *one*, the mathematical impossibility which, in literature, seemed was possible anyway. What he wanted to know was *how*.

David got out of bed, washed his hands and face, brushed his teeth, and stumbled toward the kitchenette of his studio apartment to put some yogurt and granola in a bowl and place a coffee capsule in his espresso machine. He sat, as he did each morning, at the window and watched people cross 14th St. He remembered his idea that Sancho Panza and Don Quixote were one and the same person and again thought about *one* being *two. In a way*, he thought, *aren't we all more than one person?*

Later, walking out into the street and seeing people dressed up for Halloween, the idea felt less self-evident than it had a few minutes earlier. *Sure, we're all more than one person*, he continued his thought, *but that's on the inside. Outside we're still stuck with the limits of our bodies. We can't just will our bodies to shift shape and become someone else. That's why we have to wear masks.* But arriving at Union Square, where the subway station was filling with people, he realized this idea wasn't so simple either. *People pierce themselves*, he thought, *they tattoo themselves, they get injections, surgeries. Isn't this all about being able to be more than one person?*

The thought bothered him as he went down into the subway station, walked through the pedestrian tunnels to the 4 train, and, at the last minute – just before the doors closed – managed to squeeze into one of the cars going uptown to Hunter College, where he taught a class on trends in literature.

Can we really be two people? he thought as the train clanked uptown. *If we feel like two people, then it means there's a split inside, and we try to heal that split, with either psychological or surgical means. Sancho Panza and Don Quixote* cannot *be the same person,* he decided. *It's a logical impossibility. They* have *to be two separate people.*

The train arrived at 68th St. and David got out of the car. He walked with the crowds up the stairs and looked at the people around him. Most of them had dressed up for Halloween – more than he would have expected. *I used to love Halloween,* he thought to himself. *Why hadn't it occurred to me to dress up?*

David entered the West Building and went up the elevator to his office on the thirteenth floor. He walked down the hallway, unlocked the door, and sat down at his desk. He needed to prepare for class and had an idea -- to connect the lesson plan to Halloween. He was teaching *Invitation to a Beheading* by Nabokov and he thought of painting a red bright line in lipstick across his neck. He got up and was about to step out of his office to see if anyone on the floor had lipstick he could borrow -- but then he stopped himself. *I can't,* he thought, *teach an entire class with lipstick across my neck! The students won't be able to focus!*

David went back to preparing for class, reading back over the passages he liked most, and about thirteen minutes before class was supposed to start he got up, took his book and lecture notes in hand, and went to the elevator. Julie, who taught a graduate seminar on transnationality at the same time, was standing next to the elevator. She looked up at David and chuckled. *Hello Julie,* David said, and Julie said, *Hi David, that's really funny.* David asked her what she thought was funny and she said she liked the red mark on his neck. David instinctually put his finger up to his neck, though he knew that there was nothing there, but when looked down, saw it was streaked bright red. *Wow!* he said and, looking over at Julie, compensated with a light laugh. *I hadn't realized,* he said, *it was so bright.* She gave an understanding nod. *I think it's cool,* she said, *but I wonder whether the students will be able to focus.* David nodded back. *You're right,* he said, *I'll wash it off.* She nodded again. *It might be better . . . though I do like the idea.*

The elevator arrived and they both went inside. He pressed nine and she pressed seven. He looked up at the ceiling while she looked down at the floor. Soon the elevator stopped and the doors opened. David got off and went straight for the bathroom. The washing stations had been paperless for some months, so he went into one of the stalls to pull some toilet paper from the roll. Sticking the book under his arm, he went to the sink, wet the paper, squeezed soap onto it, and was about to rub his neck when, looking up at the mirror, he saw that his neck was clean. He looked around to see if anyone was there to see his surprise -- but he was alone. He looked at his watch and saw that he was going to be late to class. It was supposed to start in a thirteen seconds.

David rushed from the bathroom to the classroom -- and when he arrived the class was full. He had over forty students, and it was always a little hard to teach such big groups, but he made the best of it and tried to get them to at least speak in class. He saw that they'd all brought their books today and were waiting for him to begin. As he walked toward the podium, he saw a student chuckle, and another, and then another few. They were all looking straight at him and trying to hold in their chuckles. David suspected he knew what was happening and he smiled at the students. Happy Halloween! he said, and they all smiled and said, Happy Halloween! David brought his finger to his neck to see whether it was streaked with red yet again. But when he looked down he saw that his finger was clean. He looked up at the students and they were still holding in their chuckles.

We like your costume, one of the students finally said. *Totally,* said another, *it's really cool you care so much about literature.* A third said, *This is definitely the coolest thing a professor here has done.* David smiled, still not knowing how he should answer, and tried to think of something to say. *Literature is my life,* he said finally, *I have to take it seriously, but I also have to know how to take it lightly.* The students all agreed and, with that, he was able to start his lecture.

The class went well, he felt, and when it was over he wished everyone a Happy Halloween again. A young student whose name David did not know came up and asked him to clarify something he'd said earlier. After David had explained his point, he asked the student what he thought David was supposed to be for Halloween. *It's obvious,* said the student chuckling, *you're Don Quixote.* Another student -- a young woman whose name David didn't know either -- overheard the first student as she was walking out and turned to say, *No he's not, man, he's Sancho Panza!*

David took a step back, trying to laugh, but saw that they had both turned serious. *He's Don Quixote,* said the young man, and the young woman said, *That's crazy, how can he be Don Quixote when he's totally Sancho Pan-*

za? David tried to mediate between them, saying, *Maybe I'm both*, but they both huffed. *Sancho Panza and Don Quixote can't be the same person*, said the young woman, and the young man nodded, *Yeah, professor, you can't have Don Quixote be Sancho Panza, the whole point is that they aren't the same person.* Having found agreement, the two students left, and David found himself in the classroom alone. Instead of leaving and going back up to his office he fell into one of the seats and sank down.

I'm losing myself, he said to himself, and then added, *I'm turning into a logical impossibility.* His insides twisted in pain. *What am I supposed to do about this situation? he asked out loud.*

What situation? he heard Julie's voice.

Startled, he said, *My costume situation. No one knows who I'm supposed to be for Halloween. Including myself.*

Isn't it obvious? Julie asked.

Is it? he asked.

You're Don Quipanza.

David tried to smile but instead felt tears welling in his eyes.

You think? he said as the tears streaked his cheeks. *I thought I was Sancho Xote.*

Julie smiled, walked over, caressed his head. *You're whoever you want to be,* she said. *You're the one who decides.*

David felt the tears flow more intensely, the pain being squeezed out, and wanted to say something, but found he'd lost his voice.

Let's catch a Halloween drink, Julie said to him. *Bedford Falls starts happy hour at noon.*

David got up and followed Julie out of the classroom, down the hall to the elevator, and out of the building. Out on the street he reached out and took her hand

-- not romantically but out of fear. He clutched her hand tight and she clutched his hand too. They had always been nice to each other, coming to each other's faculty talks, showing collegiality at meetings and events, but it had never seemed that their relationship might extend beyond their department. Now they were walking down the street hand in hand. And Julie felt to David like she would be there to defend him against all the giants and monsters that might ever try to destroy him.

David's eyes brightened as he look at the back of Julie's head. *You're the one,* he said, *you're my Don Quixote.*

She looked back, her eyes focused and her smile confident, responding, *Yes, David, and you're my Dulcinea.*

They reached Bedford Falls and went inside -- the bar full of all kinds of people dressed up in costumes for Halloween.

Is this what it's like every year? David asked. *Is everyone always out this early?*

It's Friday, October 31, said Julie, *if you switch the digits of the date around you get Friday the 13th, so people are more excitable than usual, they're taking the afternoon off to party. At least that's what I heard from some friends.*

. .

David thought he saw his two students, the ones who stayed after class, at a corner table having a beer and leaning into each other, but looking closer he seemed not to recognize their faces after all.

Julie settled David down at a table at the other corner and went over to the bar to get them drinks. *Could all three of them be the same person?* David thought to himself. *Quixote, Panza, and Dulcinea? Maybe we're all everybody and everybody is us?*

Julie came back with a pint of beer in either hand

-- but she had, in the meantime, painted her face green. David was disgusted. He was unable to look her straight in the eyes. The guardian had turned into a menace. And David's sadness turned into suspicion. It had all started, he realized, when he ran into Julie before class. Until that moment, the day had been like any other, full of thoughts and actions, but without a single hint of strangeness. She had put a spell on him, he realized, she had used some kind of enchantment. And now that he'd realized what had happened he would have to fight against it without her knowing -- else she would simply use an enchantment of a different sort.

Remind me, said David as Julie sat and put the pint glasses down on the table, *do you have a boyfriend? Are you married?*

Divorced, Julie said. *And I'm also seeing someone.*

What's his name? David asked and Julie answered, *David.*

David forced a smile as he tried to recall whether he'd forgotten that he and Julie had started seeing each other or whether it was just a new enchantment she was trying to use on him. Before he could decide which it was she lifted her pint glass and so David, too, lifted his pint glass -- and they clinked glasses.

David's glass split down the middle, the two halves falling into each other, and beer poured down and across the table. David looked down at his right hand and saw that it was bleeding -- the red drops falling on the table and mixing with the yellowed brew. Before he knew it, Julie was up and over at his side of the table, wrapping his hand in her scarf, pulling it tight to stop the bleeding as its threads filled with a deep burgundy hue. Her face, too, lost its green hue and turned burgundy like blood.

Get away, evil enchanter, he cried, *leave this castle at once, and never come back!*

Julie tried to calm David down, but he began to push her away, and people in the bar came to separate them, but when David began pushing them too, they all turned their efforts to restraining him.

I am Don David, David said, *do not touch me, or else my Dulcinea will ride over you on her donkey, and my Sancho will battle you with his helmet of Mambrino, and I will throw myself out of here on a blanket!!*

David felt himself picked up by the hands of a giant, as if he were a child, and taken out of the bar into the street, where he was put down on the sidewalk. He looked down at his hand and it was healed, a clean scarf wrapped around it, as if it was merely there to keep it warm. The sun had set outside and it was dusk, the last few rays of sun lighting up the sky behind the West Building down the block. David turned around and Julie was next to him, holding her arms out, and he hugged her stronger than he had ever hugged anyone. He felt himself missing everyone he'd ever loved, until Julie herself became all these people, and David, too, became all these people, and he wondered whether we were all actually nothing other than everyone we ever loved.

This was, he finally understood, the sense in which they were all -- Don Quixote and Sancho Panza and Dulcinea de Toboso and all the others – actually the same person.

As she continued to hug him with one arm, Julie put out the other arm and hailed a cab -- until one finally stopped at the curb. She opened the door for David and he sank into the cab seat, and when the driver asked him where he said, in tears, *I don't know.* Julie got into the cab and told the driver to take them to Queens, across from Astoria Park, where she lived just next to Hell Gate Bridge.

By the time they arrived it was dark, and as Julie led David upstairs to her apartment, he noticed that her body had begun to glow with a kind of radiance that seemed rooted in the simplest of acts that anyone had ever performed -- caring. He saw his own failure at that moment in the clearest of lights, recalling he'd forgotten to tell his students what pages they were supposed to read for next week, and promising himself that he would send them a message the next morning with all the information. He also promised himself that he would be good to Julie -- that he would repay her for her care with care of his own -- and that, from now until death came between them, they would read books and talk about them together.

David was barely conscious as Julie laid him down on a wide couch, put an old quilt over him, and settled his head into a broad pillow that seemed as soft as it was big. *We'll read books together,* he mumbled as his consciousness slipped away, and as it did, he wondered whether it was actually death itself, already, coming to separate them forever -- before the two of them had had time to read together even a single book.

- David Stromberg

FLYING LESSON

We kissed a long goodbye in the hotel lobby
as the cab curled into the driveway.
Athens stoplights blinked their farewells
in the 3:00 am darkness, speeding me
to the airport. You will fly the same plane,
same flight, same seat in a week after
your Greek party cruise with girlfriends.
In seat 26D I scribbled lavish lines
to you, tucked the poem under my cushion
above the life vest. I was certain no one cleans
a 777 well enough to find and toss love notes.
My email told you where to find my message
that began with I love. Your email
reply began with I can't--

- Alan Perry

Herbert Cantly hadn't really wanted to get up before seven, an ungodly hour for him, the morning of their final day in Paris. His sleep problems, really his norm lately, hadn't improved his willingness to be driven to some out-of-the way gardens in the boonies. But his wife, Jessy, though also groggy, was excited about seeing where Monet had lived, painted, and nurtured his paradise. Corinne, their ebullient chauffeur and tour guide for this Thursday – a French friend of an old friend of the Clantys, back in Connecticut – had picked up the couple from their timeshare apartment at eight am, the hour, she said, they needed to leave to avoid the worst of the late July crowds at Giverny.

Before exiting Paris, Corinne pulled up to a worn little house in the 7th arrondissement, not far from Saint-Germain, where the other two American passengers got in her spacious red Renault. The second couple, seated up front next to the driver, greeted Corinne with kisses and, in Herbert's opinion, over-the-top enthusiasm, and paid scant attention to the Cantlys. Sterling and Georgie seemed a lot more awake than the visitors from across the sea, who let them set the tone and substance of the conversation for most of that day. They both went on at some length, mostly with Corinne, about the week-long yoga retreat they'd just attended in Gironde.

"It was just sheer transcendence," said Sterling.

"Except it didn't do anything, unfortunately, to ease my back pain," said Georgie.

Herbert took an almost immediate dislike to Sterling, who was very blond, very tall, tanned, lean, and muscled – quite unlike Herbert, whom Jessy called, only in private of course, pleasantly pudgy. He also pictured himself as well, when trying to be objective, rather bland in both appearance and disposition. Herbert paid less attention, initially, to Sterling's dark--haired wife, almost a foot shorter than her husband, and who, at least from Herbert's back seat vantage, looked to be pleasing in both form and features – nose perhaps a bit aquiline, maybe a bit on the plump side, hard to tell in her shapeless smock. They arrived in Giverny around ten a.m., each paying their ten euros admission, and entered Claude Monet's domain, little changed, their guide book told them, since the artist lived there for two score years a century ago.

Their explorations of both the house and gardens, under bright enervating sun, took about two hours. Although Georgie had been there before, she, like Jessy, oohed and aahed about the unconstrained flowerbeds and the vast water garden. But, Herbert, uncertain whether he knew the difference between Monet and Manet, and annoyed by the chattering hordes of chirpy, picture snapping Chinese or Japanese tourists, he couldn't tell which, dutifully following their guides with the signal flags, would have been happy to depart Monet's paradise after sixty minutes. He exited the tour prematurely when their guide got to the separate upstairs bedrooms of Claude and wife Alice, informing Jessy that he was going downstairs to sit on the porch.

Slumped in an uncomfortable wooden chair, Herbert reflected on Sterling's take-charge persona, his superior view of himself and his "transcendent" adventures into the higher spirit life. To his surprise and annoyance, Sterling soon joined him on the porch, saying he'd been at Giverny several times before, and didn't like house tours, even homes of great artists.

Turned out that Sterling just wanted to enthuse more about the wonders of their yoga retreat. Even though, despite her expectations, Georgie had found no relief from her nagging back pains – which began the previous year when she fell off her bicycle into a passing truck. His juices warmed up, and apparently expecting little response from Herbert, Sterling proceeded, with equal enthusiasm, to talk about the spiritual path both he and Georgie had embarked upon, after his earlier years peddling various medications in places like Djakarta and Abu Dhabi. Buddhist Right Action, the Eightfold Path, Karma, reincarnation. Transcendence." Herbert wished he could just find a cozy little sofa somewhere and take a nap.

At lunch, in a flower-adorned café just a few hundred feet from the garden entrance, Georgie recommended the terrine. So they all ordered terrine, pâté, and cheeses, before talking, for a few minutes, initially, about what was going on back in the States.

Jessy said they were heartened by what Obama had accomplished in his first two years.

"Oh yeah," said Sterling, "he's a great orator, I'll grant you. But, my God, still those endless wars, rotten health care insurance, great inequality in money, race, and so. We'll wait a while, thank you, before we pay another visit to the States."

Trying to veer in another direction, Georgie told the vacationers that she and Sterling meditated each morning for an hour. "It helps de-clutter your brain and soul."

"Helps us focus," added Sterling.

Jessy said, after a moment, "We play Scrabble every afternoon."

"I read," Georgie deadpanned, "that playing Scrabble can help delay the onset of Alzheimer's." After another brief time of silence all around, she asked, "But do you and Herbert have any spiritual practices?"

"Actually," said Jessy with a trace of vehemence, "we're quite conventional liberal but conflicted Catholics, like some of our friends. Hoping for the best, for meaningful reform, change. But we're not ready to give up the Eucharist. And all the trappings."

"They help us find," interjected Herbert, entering the skirmish, "what'd you call it, Sterling? Transcendence!"

"Well, different strokes, as they say. You know, Herbert, I had one hell of a road to Damascus experience about ten years ago,"

"After you left Big Pharma," added Georgie.

"And my marriage," Sterling added. "Georgia left hers too. We make ends meet, nowadays, by a variety of odd jobs. Translating, music transcription, teaching something or other from time to time. It's allowed us to lead our nomadic existence in a number of interesting countries. We'll likely stay in Paris a bit longer, in our rented house, until the universe leads us somewhere else. Right, Georgie?"

His wife nodded. "My trust fund helps."

"And we both left your universal RC church," said Sterling with a chuckle, continuing the tale of his odyssey. "We gave up all those myths, those conventions, those absurd, stifling, puritanical ideas. And now we're really free. And getting freer every moment. Aren't we, Georgie? "

"Truly," replied Georgie, with an almost beatific smile. "Except for this damn pain in my back. I need to take ten to twelve pills a day just to keep going. My supply's running very low, and my doctor's on vacation in China for the next month."

"What kind of pills?, " asked Herbert.

"Hydrocodone. Oxy. Others."

"Oh yeah, OxyContin. We got just a few of them,

but a lot of others. They give us more little plastic bottles every time we get a dental extraction, or a root canal. Or minor surgeries. We hardly ever need them. They're piled up in one of our drawers at home. For a rainy day, I suppose."

"Do you think you could kindly spare a few dozen, Herbert? If you have that many?"

"Sure. I guess so," said Herbert. "Why not? We'll mail you three or four dozen as soon as we get home."

Returning to Paris, Corinne suggested, for some religious diversity, that they all go to the Jewish Museum before it closed for the day, and then to the Saint-Paul-Saint-Louis Church in Marais. "My late husband and I sometimes attended Mass there."

Herbert begged off, He was pooped, and just needed to chill out for a while. Saying she needed to do a few vital household chores, Georgie invited Herbert to recuperate at their home until the travelers returned at nightfall.

"I really appreciate you're sending me four dozen of whatever pills you got,." said Georgie, after they were dropped off at her house. Following a round of iced gin-and-tonics, Georgie excused herself to bestow some much-needed water on her garden, turning on the TV, so Herbert could watch football, of the French variety.

Coming inside after only a few minutes, complaining of the heat, and getting them another round of drinks, Georgie asked Herbert if he'd like to try out the hot tub with her. "You can use a pair of Sterling's trunks, if you need to."

Putting the TV on mute, Herbert said he'd just rather keep relaxing indoors,

After several minutes of silence between them, Georgie said "You're not too keen on Sterling, are you?"

"I barely know your husband."

"He's not my husband. So tell me, please. What's your first impression?"

"We're not soulmates." He hesitated after that announcement. "He's too self-assured for my taste. Too full of himself. But, as he told us at the restaurant, 'different strokes.'"

"He often does suck all the air out of the room. But he has his share of doubts, insecurities. He didn't mention that, in addition to his failed marriage, there were two little boys. He hasn't seen them for years." She stopped, looking thoughtfully out the widow towards her garden, "That's why he goes on that way. We understand each other."

Herbert was silent, uncomfortable with this information, bothered, but simultaneously pleased, by Georgie's sharing with him her husband's secrets. He told himself that he was all the things that Sterling wasn't. He was glad of that, he assured himself.

"You know," she said after a few minutes, "what Sterling said about being free of restrictions, puritanical inhibitions. We have a pretty open relationship. It's okay what we do with others, so long as we don't shove it in each other's face."

Unsure of how to reply, he again muttered, "different strokes," wishing he could come up with some fresher catchphrase.

"For instance, he and Corinne ..."

His mind racing, confused by where this conversation was going, Herbert turned to the silent TV, trying to watch the silent ghostlike figures on the screen racing up and down the field.

"I need to cool off," she said, suddenly standing up and tugging her shapeless garment over her head, revealing, to his surprise and wonder, her teeless, braless, firm, and erect breasts.

Trying not to gape, Herbert's head swiveled again to the TV..

Bending her body down towards his face, moving shakily, perhaps because of the gin, Georgie glanced at his lap and laughed. "I guess you're not so tired now, are you?"

Herbert looked down too, as both observed the sudden bulge on his lap.

"Okay, Herbie," she said, pulling him up from the sofa, "it's time for us to take a little spiritual journey of our own, before the weary pilgrims return."

"You really don't have to do this just because I'm sending you some pain killers."

"I'm actually not that transactional, sweet Herbie." she said. "It's just one kindness for another." Beckoning toward the worn steps leading upstairs, Georgie showed the way to the little bedroom. He followed her, a little woozy, but, he felt, less and less confused. She closed the door behind them.

* * *

"There must be close to 250," said Herbert, back in Milford, the following Sunday, after Mass, and Pad Thai at Lucky Rice Bowl restaurant, as they sat at the kitchen table counting. "Vicodin, Toprol, Darvacet, Tramadol, OxyContin. "I never heard of half of them. We'll never use them. It'd be a kindness to help relieve someone's pain."

"You realize she's most likely an addict," said Jessy. "Even if she didn't make up that sad tale about falling off her bike."

"She doesn't look like an addict to me."

"Okay, Mr. Expert, then just give her your pills. I

don't want to be her enabler,"

"I'll send her a hundred now. Maybe more later."

"Good. Then you can keep up your correspondence with her." Trying for a more positive note, Jessy asked, "You know the best part of our trip for me? Beside Notre Dame? Giverny. The lush lily ponds, those bridges covered with wisteria. That cute country restaurant. Paradise on earth. How about you?"

"Yeah, the gardens" he said, picturing, not for the first time in the last few days, Georgie's tanned body next to him in bed, trying not to think about the guilt feelings already beginning to enfold him, "A great experience. To quote Sterling, 'transcendent!'"

- Gerald Kamens

TAPPAN ZEE BRIDGE

Beatrice stood on the Tappan Zee Bridge. She looked onto the Hudson River through milky gray membranes. Dark and light shapes of water shifted hundreds of feet below. Tittering serpent waves with silk tongues promised a landing as soft as a feather pillow.

Dirty air circled the webbing of her brain. It touched the vibrant memory of Stan's fat unibrow like a caterpillar mulching grass. On Saturday night, they'd wrestle naked, Stan's meaty calves holding her down. With each hump, it made Beatrice feel the size of a pinhole, while streaking her across the sky. That was until two months in, Stan buttoned up his corduroy shirt, pulled up his jean jeggings and said they couldn't meet anymore in the Church Rec Room.

It's not a moralistic decision, Stan said.

They used the Rec Room since they both lived at home and Stan's mom was the organist and he had keys. Sandy from their Writing Comp class at Westchester Community College had asked Stan to be her boyfriend, and he'd said yes.

Nothing personal, Stan said. *Stan and Sandy sound good together, a sea of S's, that's all.*

Her tight blonde curls sucking her neck and twitchy mouth and hips didn't hurt either. Stan didn't say the part about the curls and her twitching body, but Beatrice knew.

That morning, the sun was barely up. Beatrice liked her upside-down choice. Day starting, life ending. She hoped her limbs would break and form a floating 'S' in the water that Stan and Sandy would see, feel bad about, and then break-up. Beatrice would plague Stan's dreams from her death state. Plant earworms of sadness and regret so he couldn't cross the bridge without choking on loss through his bulbous nose and sweet thin lips. Acne bloomed on either side of Beatrice's temples like twin roses. She wiped her chubby cheeks and readied herself for the nosedive. It wasn't just Sandy. Stan had told her she was too open, wanting too much, a needy hand.

Wasn't that love, she asked?

Maybe Stan was too closed, not wanting enough, a fingerless useless hand. But a week later, his words turned her inside out. The occasional jogger who passed her on the bridge, running toward Nyack or Tarrytown, barely acknowledged her. Not even a flicker of eye contact. The thought of all the future snubs and jabs by people she didn't know yet was the final push to jump.

Clutching the arm of the bridge, something strange happened. The metal was cold under her hands, but steady. It didn't feel like she expected it to. It didn't feel anonymous. She looked up. The bridge towered over her. Plunging and rising white beams in orgasmic V's. She was so raw. She wasn't sure if her skin was still on her body. But the bridge looked back at her standing there. Saw her. No judgement. A reassuring quiet. It made her feel the size of a pinhole, while streaking her across the sky. Vibration under her feet caused ripples of shivers through her body. The bridge told her to hold on, so she did. Hours passed. They stayed together the whole windswept day. She didn't care who jogged by her going to Nyack or Tarrytown. Moon in the sky, the bridge told her to go home and sleep. As she walked back to her car, the lights of the bridge twinkled in Morse code. *Beatrice, come back tomorrow.*

She blushed.

That night, she dreamt the bridge's white wire strung her up in the shape of an X against one of its legs.

Sewage from the Hudson lapped below their embrace, but no matter. The wind stung their skins. They were cold. They were alive.

It was love at first sight.

- Jennifer Bowen Neergaard

WIDOW AT FARMER'S MARKET

Wedge of a woman
bound and contained
in a frail frame—

a wisp
of waning moon
floating
in deep space
like an angel's
blonde eyelash
fallen—

fondling red apples
as if they could love.

- Christine Andersen

MS. WHITNEY

As your backup, Ms. Whitney, your call is my response—but I'm
concerned.
Forgive me if I interrupt and over-sing my part if I sweat like a
Georgia peach,
blame Hotlanta's heat, but your ornamented, mezzo-soprano
now sounds cracked   betrayed notes flee your
melisma,
the "I" in "I'll Always Love You," unlike the blossom-filled tree,
fat birdsong, I once knew, a blue jay that learned its song early.
You, jittery, late for rehearsal; face scratched, neck bruised,
degraded perfume cloaking stench, your eyes like a preyed upon
dear,
your body, a glass pipe squeezed.

I once knew someone like you, Ms. Whitney.
He overused. Stinky weed attacked his lungs; malt liquor burned
his gut,
and sweet wine fogged his head and opened hell's gates;
on scarred knees, he sifted carpet fibers, a beige-crystal quest,
the fat man needing one more candy bar, a corned little toe,
toilet paper pulled in bunches.

You know Ms. Whitney, Winehouse drowned her contralto in
alcohol.
Michael Jackson, Hendrix, Joplin, Morrison, Presley, and Co-
bain's ghosts
would gurgle they never needed poison for art and gifted birth-
right
is to be prized, appreciated, caressed like newborns, kissed,
and like you, loved.

Perhaps you don't wear the noose I describe Ms. Whitney,
alcohol, marijuana, pills, and cocaine rope chains.

Your minds-eye may say, That stuff that happened to him
won't happen to me. BACKUP. WAS. STUPID.

Stop twenty-one days, Ms. Whitney. It's not so easy; Hurricane
winds bend palms.
You might need a rock when praying to God or your lower soul.
I'll understand when that happens. It always does with moaners
like us, notes on a staff, F below middle C.
This secret I'll share with you,
Life is better lived free of knots.
And, no, Ms. Whitney, I carry no cigarette lighter.

- Ron Dowell

Close Harmony

In the 1844 Gothic church—a marvel of stained-glass windows, gables and spires, all permanently infused with frankincense and myrrh—Julian directed the choir and played Catholic hymns. The architectural spectacle matched his personality.

These were the late 70's when religion boomed and every church employed a full-time choir director. My parish hired Julian because he played organ, sang baritone, and displayed an endearing eccentricity. He convinced the committee—especially my friend Valerie—that his charisma and youth would produce dynamic rehearsals and spectacular holy days. Julian wanted the job because the church had a booming pipe organ, a robust choir, and a decent salary. He didn't notice at first that one of the priests was especially good-looking.

I took the job as accompanist because I needed the experience.

At one of our first rehearsals, Julian swaggered in skin-tight white pants, shoulders thrown back in his Hawaiian print shirt. It was only October, but we rehearsed Christmas music. I played the tenor part on piano as aging gentlemen attempted Handel's melismas. When they faltered, Julian led them, singing too loudly. Then he switched to soprano, unselfconsciously flipping into falsetto. The singers plowed through, sopranos sharp, flat, and everything in between. My musician's ear winced, but Julian had persuaded the choir to accept his challenge and I realized he wouldn't allow them to fail.

I heard chuckling and looked up. Julian had jumped to the top of a desk. He swayed, arms flung wide, eyes rolled back, seemingly immersed in musical rapture.

Valerie looked amused and triumphant.

A few weeks later, Julian chattered about a date.

"Where did you go?" I said.

Turns out they stayed in. It seemed out of character—Julian loved late nights and bars.

"Curt thought it best." He stopped sorting music and looked directly at me.

So, he spent the night with a priest. I tried to look liberal and open-minded.

Julian swore me to secrecy—said only Valerie and I knew. On Sundays, during the homily, Julian and I slipped out so he could tell me about Curt's dinners and gifts. I thought they might be in love, but other weeks, he talked of bars, baths, and one-night stands.

It took several years, but Julian stopped seeing Curt. A former student at the seminary himself, Julian said gay culture permeated its ranks. He never took his own vows but swore he respected Curt's.

In the early 80's, Julian shared another secret. He showed me his AZT bottles, lined up on the counter. When he told me what they cost, I wondered how he paid for them. While I tried to be hopeful, Julian dreamed of Hawaii. Warm air. Sun. A permanent vacation. As though life was short, and he must get somewhere fast to live it. It only took a few months to submit his resume and land a gig in Honolulu. He promised to call every week and return for regular visits.

Every Sunday, I pictured him at the organ, Plumeria scent blowing through open windows. He would convince his choir that singing cantatas and chorales was the most precious experience of their lives.

We worked around time zones to settle on an 11 p.m. phone time, and then, once or twice a week, Julian painted me word pictures of his lanai, the ocean breeze across his face, his musical triumphs at the organ.

When he could afford it, he flew to Wisconsin. On one visit, we ate schnitzel at a gasthaus with his mother, sister, and our friend Valerie. I expected Julian to shock us with an absurd story or profanity. But he made Valerie talk about her children and begged his mother to describe her Mother's Day flowers.

Someone mentioned sweets and he turned. Then his torso twitched. I laid a hand on his arm. "Julian?" He leaned away and toppled. I felt the room collapse and imagined diners frozen, forks immobile above plates of bratwurst.

While Julian seized, a waiter's voice echoed. "Yes, an ambulance. A heart attack." I suppose it looked like a heart attack, but we at the table recognized a seizure, not uncommon in AIDS patients.

Distant sirens. Red lights outside the window. Men in blue uniforms. Medical bags.

Julian refused a hospital visit but did relinquish his car keys. Valerie drove him to his mother's house while I followed in my own car, a somber two-car procession. We held his arms as he walked the porch stairs and settled him on the couch where he slept the rest of the day.

In the remaining days, he longed for Hawaii, dismissing my concerns about his ability to endure a 10-hour flight. At least in this stubbornness, he seemed himself.

At first, when he returned, he wrote of islanders, luaus, flowers, and feasts. But soon, he spoke of court papers and invoices. He spent too much on a boyfriend, furniture, a trip to Italy, medications. A lawyer filed his bankruptcy petition. He must have sensed my disapproval, but he simply reminded me that AIDS patients have only months or years.

In his final days, Julian was too weak or delirious

for letters or calls, so I talked to his boyfriend, David. Days would go by without news, and then David called to say he was gone.

I returned the phone to its cradle and gravitated to my piano, where I pulled out one of our favorite hymns. But under me, the bench felt like stone, the notes on the page a watery blur, and the melody out of tune, like a string had fallen from the works.

- Nancy Jorgenson

DESPERATE LOVE

At any one time we usually have a nest or two in the branches of the oak trees in our front yard. Mourning doves, grackles, mockingbirds. On various occasions I have happened upon a fledgling. A sparsely feathered creature hopping and cheeping, and I have to suppress the desire to intervene. I know this is part of their journey to independence—maturity.

Sometimes certain offspring are kicked out too soon. I have on more than one occasion come across the shriveled corpse of a nestling along my front walk. Wings at an angle, feathers still yolked together. I can't help but imagine the crimes for such an early dismissal: eating too much or too little, not practice preening or wanting to get preened. What was it that became too much to manage? Threatened the survival of the whole brood.

Her love was a physical love. The nipping and pecking of fingers, affectionate squeezes and the sing-song voice. *Cosquillas y hermosuras susurrando en mi corazón.* As long as we were united in purpose: the validation of her love. Non-corroboration meant falling out of favor.

I remember slipping between my parents in bed, two solid walls of protection, on nights when I couldn't sleep. Nights when the dreams were so bad I didn't want to close my eyes. Nights when making a pallet on the floor beside the bed was not enough to chase the phantoms from my vision.

It was warm. Between their bodies, both bigger than mine, nestled under their quilt, softer than mine. With each of their backs to me I could finally close my eyes and breathe deep as I waited for sleep.

When I was older, I stopped sneaking into their room, stopped calling out for my dad to carry me over the crawling bodies and creeping hands I was sure would loom out of the darkness the second my feet hit carpet. It was then that my mom offered to harbor me. My father went out of town a lot. He traveled to different school districts around the state auditing their performance and consulting on improvements. On these nights she asked me to fill his spot in her half-empty bed.

She would find my hand in the darkness. Sometimes twine her legs in mine. That same quilt feels too thick, as the air feels too thick now.

My body is folded under my aunt's legs. Covered by her colcha. The air is still, and my back is stiff from want of uncurling. It was Christmas, a cold one at that, and she was susceptible to respiratory illness. When she invited me under the woven wrap, I felt uncomfortable but couldn't speak the word no. She was kind enough, but not the kind of aunt that invited such closeness.

This aunt and uncle on my father's side, my three cousins lived in Harlingen and we traveled once a month and most holidays to see them. They lived more free-range lives. Their R.V. sat in the small plot right next to my grandparents' house, both leading out to the canal. No fence or road of separation. Hide-and-seek was a free-for-all that could last well after sunset. Round after round of counting and running for the next new spot, the one where you hoped to be last found, winner. The adults gathered in my grandparents' living room as we played. I ran inside searching for an unused gem of a spot when my aunt called me over.

"Come here," she said. "Get under my chair."

I could hear my cousin calling ready or not and slipped under her seat. Behind her legs, beneath her blanket. My back rounded, head to knees, arms around legs to scrunch in tighter, I fit perfectly. The adults continued their conversation. I heard quick stomping feet travel in and out of the rooms, doors slamming open and shut.

"Have you seen Missy?"

"You know you have to find her yourself," my uncle said.

Time passed and I felt the sweat collecting along my neck, behind my knees. I itched to raise my head, straighten my legs. I wondered when my aunt would give me up. I didn't want to reveal my spot, but I didn't think I could last much longer. I couldn't bring myself to let her down or shirk her help. Even for sweet release.

I slip one leg out, relishing the cool on my skin. And like this I could make it through the night. Eventually, even on nights when my dad was home, her bed was half-empty. My younger sister and I took turns filling the dad-shaped hole.

I couldn't always trust her words, but I could her body. I don't know what she'll say, but I know I can reach for her. Minor slip ups—a lost bracelet, the breaking of a dish—can be laughed off or met with contention. "Are you dumb? Don't you know how to listen?" To question her is to spin the wheel of invocation: silence, anger, guilt. "I might as well kill myself since no one cares what I have to say." I'm at a loss at times for which actions will call her to defend my independence. "She should be able to date. I'll chaperone," she tells my father. Which invite disgust. "Do you really like girls?" The words drip from her lips like the water beading off my naked skin in the shower where she chose to confront me.

I know when we walk I can hold her hand. I know I can rub her feet and check her scalp for dry skin, and I am welcomed in her space. I know she can randomly put me on her legs and lift me up and down on the lever she creates even when I am too big for it.

And I loved so freely with my own body. Even when I push away, have to flit the quilted cocoon to stretch my aching muscles, I curl back into this love that is warm and familiar, consuming, home. I know what I feel is what she says on the phone when she thinks I can't hear. This heat that trickles out from her lips in secret spurts and slithers into my ears. This passion building until it can be held in no longer or I'll blow. It oozes out of my body. My hands, my lips. Onto his skin.

What do you see in the mirror when you are driving us home, Mother? Do you check for traffic? Do you check for me? My body laid out along the seat, my head in his lap. Can you see his hands?

Then there are the times I can't reach her. She is closed off to me. I stand on either side of the door. I'm right here. I can feel her. The vibrations of the knocking, the pounding through the door. I want to open, but I also need some space. I can hear her. Her muffled voice, her breathing. I call out and it goes silent, still. Please let me in, but she has to keep me out.

And I have to keep them out. They know they can climb into my lap, onto my back, pick at my food, dip sips of my tea. They can be my shadows, ride my drift. But some days I find myself in the bathroom. I hear their chirruping voices, but to respond is to give away my location. I hear the hopping steps, the flutter of air as they pass my door. And I stay silent until they move on in continued search.

Their bodies, once inside me, now rest on the outside and belly to belly I feel their breath mimic my breath. Their chests rise up and fall down, rise, fall down. I watch like a hawk for a chance to unnestle. Heat and sweat, trapped between our skin, sprouts and gathers, plasters their hair, near invisible down feathers to their heads. Slips down into their folded necks. The salt and sour hold a hint of sweet when I bury my nose inside. Their breath warms my breast as they begin to suck, and I feel the warm itch that signals them to draw more, luring love and life until it burns like a tongue scraped raw, mouths demanding more than I have to give. Their smooth hands glide over my curve of skin and they squeeze and pull, occasionally prick with the nails that grow faster than I can clip them. Palms, so soft and alive, not content unless cupping, gripping, clawing my body, perch on my breast. Finally mouths and hands are still.

Their delightfully round heads rest in the crook of my arm, and belly to belly we create a warm womb, their legs tucked into mine. Their hearts pump and thump into my chest, my own personal timekeepers. Ticking away each potential moment of departure. Just as sleep starts to roost heavy on my face, they stir and their razorbill latch grips me alert, thoughts of autonomy scatter as I settle into their warmth. Into the nest of inseperate me and them. I study their chests and it is not me but my eyes that slip away—rise up and fall, rise and fall down. My body too tired to take flight.

- Melissa Nunez

I never loved Leonard. We met at a party, oh, twenty years ago now, at this self-consciously down-at-the-heel apartment. The city was so expensive that all of us young professionals felt righteously poor. Everyone there was slightly unwashed — clean kids trying to look feral, myself included. Greasy ponytail, obese father's old polo shirt over a pair of tights. I was talking with some girlfriend — I can't remember her name. Darla? Karen? She wasn't so much a friend as someone I dragged around to hide how much I preferred to be alone—when I heard this incredible barking man-laugh. I turned. In a small knot of people, a tall, floppy-haired kid was throwing back his head with unselfconscious joy. There was something about that back-of-head, that awkward height, the long wool overcoat still worn in spite of the apartment's blasting heater. I cut off my friend and announced: "You sound like a fucking seal."

The kid turned. I had bet on him being a certain attainable degree of not-that-attractive. In reality, he fell a little short. His angry face changed to pleasantly confused as he saw his attacker had breasts. "Excuse me?" he said.

In thirty seconds I had "Leonard" looming over me, stammering out his life story while I pretended to hang on every word. Lower-upper-middle class suburb in Ohio, midwestern liberal arts college, weekends playing Ultimate. I drew out what shamed him: college Republicans, born-again mother, his lone trip abroad to the Canadian side of Lake Erie. How many times had I thus compulsively confessed to some prospective romantic partner about the tests I'd cheated on, the money I'd stolen from relatives, the boyfriend to whom I'd lost my virginity sort-of-by-accident? Now it was Leonard's turn. I couldn't wait to never call him again.

But as he went on, his interest in me obviously growing, I began to feel sick. I saw it all and hated it already: the excuses we'd make to go home together, the kissing and fumbling removal of clothes, the vulnerability of our not-very-recently-washed bodies. Finally, unable to stop myself, I said, "Can I ask you a blunt question?"

Leonard blushed, God bless him, from scalp to neckline. "Sure."

"Do you ever lie awake at night and wonder why you shouldn't throw yourself out the window?"

He screwed up his eyebrows, as though with sufficient force he could use them to extract the small, bad thing from inside of me. "What?" he said. "No. Do you?"

"No," I said, like when Mom asked if I'd seen the money she kept in the Altoids tin.

Leonard glanced at the door. A group of people, not the same people he'd been talking to, were putting on their coats and boots. "Listen," he said. "My friends are taking off. Do you have a ride?"

"Need" would have been an invitation. Instead, Leonard, stupid Ohioan Leonard, was rejecting me. So be it — in my head we had already put on underwear and eaten brunch, and I was now walking down the frozen street, trash blowing around me, grateful to be alone.

"I'll wait for my friend," I said. Darla/Karen had disappeared.

"Sure," he said. "Well! It was nice to—"

"I'm not nice," I said, but he was gone.

The next morning, I went out early. It seemed important to pretend we'd gone home together and play out the morning after, so I walked to our awkward brunch. About four blocks from my apartment, the wind blew a huge piece of cardboard into my legs. I tried to step over it, but the wind was so strong, I couldn't pull it off me. People stared.

When I had finally freed myself, I ducked into a diner on the corner. The hostess led me to a booth. There, visible over the empty blue pleather banquette opposite, was Leonard. His cheeks were ruddy and fresh from a shower; he looked totally self-possessed, sitting at the next table with a mug of coffee and the paper, as his forefathers had done, no doubt, since time immemorial.

"I'm not following you," I said.

"Sure," Leonard said, although he didn't look it. "You know, I was thinking about your question. The one about—"

"Oh, that? That was a joke—"

"Okay. But you really got me thinking. Because I don't, of course. Feel like throwing myself out a window."

I considered murdering him. "But," he went on, "then I started to wonder — why? And I couldn't come up with a good answer. It's like, so obvious I can't explain it. I mean, I would miss coffee."

"Coffee?"

"Yeah. And like, all this." He held up his hands and laughed his incredibly joyous, barking laugh.

And then his face fell. Colossally, tragically. It was like watching an iceberg calve. And I could see what he was thinking: I laugh like a fucking seal.

"No!" I said. "No no no no no!" I jumped up and slid into the banquette across from him. "I totally didn't mean it. You have a great laugh. I— I was just trying to get your attention!"

"Is that the truth?" Leonard asked.

It was not. But in that moment, I would have said

or done anything — washed my hair and gone on pleas-
ant dates, gotten married in a church, pretended to like
boating in Ohio — if it meant that, for the rest of his life,
Leonard could laugh his awful laugh in perfect unself-
conscious freedom.

"Yes," I said. "In fact: I love your laugh."

The waitress came. She brought coffee and little
plastic tubs of fake creamer. It was a good diner.

Leonard gave me a shy smile.

"You'd miss it, too, you know," he said. "Coffee. If
you really thought it through."

"I think you're right," I said.

But inside, I was saying: I'll learn to love you.

And I will. One day, Leonard, I will.

- *Lauren Schenkman*

BROWN-EYED GIRL

I'm a sucker for traditional romance. Flowers and love notes? Yes, please. Kissing scenes in movies? Bring it. So it makes perfect sense that I should marry a man who thinks romance is un-balling his dirty socks before throwing them on the floor or disposing of his pistachio shell cairns within 48 hours. When he does do romantic things, like playing my favorite song or building an Ikea monstrosity, it's great. It's always a surprise. But then there are the other things I want him to do that I can predict, like not hate Valentine's Day. I can safely forecast I will not get what I want in these instances. My husband is a great guy with many gifts. He's smart, funny and not too proud to walk a toy poodle around the block. Romance just isn't always his thing.

He doesn't notice when I get a haircut or wear a new outfit. He isn't a flower guy and harbors an inordinate amount of resentment toward Valentine's Day. I eventually came to terms with these facts and tried putting a shine on what he does do—like fixing broken things and killing scary bugs. He's good to my family and kind to animals. He once helped me rescue a dove named Dave, even though he'd be just as likely to shoot him during hunting season. He does our taxes and our plumbing and doesn't get mad when I screw up my computer, which I do regularly.

So I'm tempted to ask, "in light of all of that, who really needs candlelight?" But I know that the answer is, "for some reason, I do."

* * *

Bill is a man of action, not sentiment. He may not whisper sweet nothings in my ear, but he will crawl under the house to install a washer and dryer so I no longer have to

155

wrestle my way through the laundromat (then he'll leave his sweaty clothes next to the washing machine). We may not go out on regular date nights, but he will act as my chauffeur around town because he knows I hate to drive. It may seem romantic that he stops what he's doing to dance with me whenever "Brown-Eyed Girl" comes on because he thinks it's our song. (It's not our song.) Still, he has his moments.

He once spent a week learning how to tumble down a blinding white mountain because he knew how much I missed skiing. After his first lesson, we rode up the swaying chairlift to a beginner's slope so he could try out his new skills. A dismount on skis is a scary proposition for any new skier, so I gave Bill plenty of clearance as we exited the lift. Apparently it wasn't enough though, because he crashed into me and wound up in the most dreaded of skier positions—under the chairlift. Once he was freed from the metal workings, I became Bill's true north. Like a magnet with goggles, he rammed into me over and over, no matter where I stood.

I tried staying with him during our descent but found it safer if I—and everyone else on the mountain—went ahead and waited for him at the bottom. As the minutes ticked by, I asked a passing skier if she'd seen a short furry man somewhere above. She replied with a proper English accent, "I passed a gentleman who toppled over and was crawling in the direction of a ski." That would be my husband.

There was the trip to Belize where he got seasick learning to scuba dive. Bill's not the strongest swimmer, but he eventually made it below the water's surface and churned along in his own unique way. There's nothing more endearing than a grown man swimming upright like a seahorse.

Romance displays itself in unlikely ways. He once

had a gig doing technical drawings for a performance by a famous musician. (Spoiler: It was Beck.) At one point the drawing stopped so Bill could produce my niece's Bat Mitzvah video. And now a Hollywood stage manager refers to my husband as "Uncle Bill."

He attends every event, performance, holiday, wedding, and family function. He isn't afraid to confront credit card statements or broken dishwashers, and he's definitely the cheapest IT guy I've ever met. He tolerates my tendency to "hobby-hop," even when it means purchasing expensive equipment I only use once, and he rarely rubs in the fact that I spent $400 building a garden which produced three green beans and a radish.

Sometimes Bill goes along with my romantic ideas. Like the time we laid out blankets and pillows on the front lawn so we could watch a meteor shower. It was freezing and we didn't see very many shooting stars, but it was pretty romantic lying in his arms. That is, until our neighbor, Ed, came by. Then it was just awkward.

Once, when we were visiting his childhood home in Waco, we slept in the same bed he did when he was growing up. There we were, two intertwined lovers in a twin-sized bed, holding tightly to each other for fear of tumbling onto the floor. Now we have a king-sized bed that all but fills our bedroom, and we wave goodnight to each other from opposite sides of the mattress. What a difference 25 years and a few dozen pounds can make.

It Happens Every Year
The wedding anniversary isn't so much a celebration as it is a case of selective amnesia. Anniversary gifts are the worst—there's so much expectation to get something with just the right sentiment—something that tells the other, "I love you. You are important to me. I want to remind you of this." Which is why Bill and I approach

the annual celebration of our commitment like a bomb disposal unit—very carefully, with the understanding that we might not make it out alive. The pressure to find the most meaningful representation of our love is overwhelming, and since neither Bill nor I is clairvoyant, every year is a crapshoot.

On our first anniversary, Bill gave me a beautiful piece of raku pottery. I loved that pot with its iridescent glaze so much that he gave me another piece for my birthday. And one for Hanukkah. I thought about telling him my pottery collection was complete. The next year he surprised me with a frosted glass vase. I considered launching into the uncomfortable "I have enough breakable containers" talk but held my tongue. Six months later, he wrapped up my vase and gave it to a relative for her birthday. I didn't know whether to be angry or relieved. I chose relieved.

Our fourth anniversary was a disaster. We took a three- and-a-half hour drive to the coast for a long weekend at the beach. One day while window shopping, I admired some beautiful emerald necklaces. Later on, Bill snuck back to the store and purchased one for me. He figured the biggest was the best, so that's the one he bought. I found it a little gaudy and would have preferred something more subtle, but I didn't know how to tell him that. I ended up just getting angry and lashing out for no apparent reason. Strangely, the whole fiasco was based on the fact that I didn't want to hurt his feelings by asking him to return the necklace and buy one I liked more. It broke my heart to think of hurting him, so instead, I just acted like a horrible person and hurt him anyway. We ended up exchanging the necklace, but I've never been able to wear it without feeling like a total schmuck.

We finally learned our lesson and gave up on anniversary gifts altogether. Coincidentally, we no longer go to bed angry on May 28th. There's usually an exchange of cards, and sometimes flowers make an appearance, but that's about it. We have our traditional sushi dinner, followed by a trip through the Krispy Kreme drive-thru. After stuffing ourselves with doughnuts and watching a little TV, we head off to bed for a steamy night of indigestion and doughnut farts, which is about as much romance as this couple can handle.

Marriage is a Verb

Romance is one thing; love is something else—like how Bill took care of me for years when I was incapacitated with chronic migraines and could barely work. He sat by my hospital bedside while I endured treatments, then spent another two years driving between Austin and Houston for ongoing appointments.

He stuck by me through the terrifying time before my diagnosis with bipolar disorder and during the following years spent in therapy trying to undo all the misery I'd caused—and there was a lot of it. This period of our marriage was decidedly unromantic—because romance's counterpoint is reality. A relationship incubates under a warm blanket of necessary fantasies we uphold as a couple. But when brutal winds blow the blanket away, our naked existence in the world is revealed, and we are left shivering beside the person we've chosen to love.

My husband could have had a much easier arrangement with a different partner—a physically and mentally stable, fun, laid-back person without weird phobias or attention deficit disorder or psoriasis or a muffin top. Instead, he chose me—an imperfect woman with an imperfect past and a questionable future. You could almost say it was romantic.

-Ilene Haddad

He Gave Himself Death

In France, when someone commits suicide, they say *Il s'est donné la mort,* He gave himself death. Surviving family and friends find comfort in the idea that suicide is a choice. Police and fire brigade come to affirm the death. There is extra administrative paperwork, often a closed coffin.

He adored the fig jam that his wife made lovingly from the figs in their garden. She had made a supply of it before the cancer claimed her. We imagine him, a year later, coming to the last pot, opening it thoughtfully rather than sadly. He was one to soldier on, which he did: living alone, shopping alone, visiting the library often, buying books very often, greeting rare visitors with joy to talk about the latest book he was reading. He often pressed books on us as we left, handing each one over with both hands, recommending it warmly.

He lived on without her and without her excellent cooking. He ignored the internet encroaching on everything. His house was silent. The television his wife had loved – especially noisy variety shows – sat mute in its corner. He continued his interests in armchair travel, cultural and historical exploration, languages, essays, theories.

Once, long ago, during summer holidays in their old house in the mountains, it rained heavily and several families plus children and friends congregated indoors to drink and talk and laugh. He became famous on that occasion for sitting in one of the cars under torrential rain, working on a book of Sanskrit. When teased about it, he smiled.

Another summer, he became obsessed with herbs, wandered the countryside collecting plants that he put into a large journal, with photos and drawings and notes. They teased him forever about that period because

160

he gave them the wrong dosage of a home-made herbal tea, and they all got diarrhea.

He was old enough to have been sent to the war in Algeria, and was there at the same time as a man who later became an extreme-right politician. 'He was a jack-ass, even back then,' he said.

A wonderful teacher, he was enthusiastic about everything, loving fieldwork, expert at tracking and stalking. His friends and fellow teacher-training students bore the nicknames of wild animals.

The finally-silent piano was forested with black and white photos of their wedding, a solemn procession of bride and groom followed by their guests through narrow Mediterranean village streets of stone houses to the town hall, the girls in high heels and bright dresses with huge stiff underskirts, the men looking sheepish in suits they would never wear again. He had outlived most of them.

She always called their figs figues blanches. The word fig has many origins: from Occitan figa, from Latin fica. He explained to her how they were pollinated but she had no patience with the technical names for things that the fig wasps did to pollinate, rubbing their bellies on the flowers before laying their eggs and dying. She laughed heartily and lost the thread as he told her about male wasps emerging through holes they chewed before depositing semen for the females, later returning to make the holes big enough to release the remaining female wasps who then had 48 hours to find a suitable tree to spread the pollen and lay eggs before dying in their turn. How she laughed.

For their honeymoon they went to the Jordan valley north of Jericho to visit the place where the first cultivated figs were found, predating the cultivation of cereals, a village dating from a dozen millennia ago. 'The first agriculture was figs,' he told her. 'They spread from the Middle East to Greece. Aristotle talks of fig trees that bear fruit and fig trees that merely help another fig tree to bear fruit. Ancient Greek farmers tied one tree to the other to help the process.' He told her that the Haggadah says the Tree of Knowledge in the Garden of Eden bore figs, not apples, that the fig is associated with sexual enlightenment hence the mention in Genesis of the fig leaf – or an apron of them – and much later the Catholic Church's 'fig leaf campaign.' She laughed, because she was not a thinker but a doer, more interested in cooking him good food, making good jam and good love.

When she was gone, late enough in a life but all too soon for him, he stayed on in their house alone. He managed. He read and reflected and put up with an isolation made worse by a pandemic. Until finally he could stay no longer, or the medics gave him bad news or a health warning or he could see a future of not-managing or, perhaps more than anything, the longing for her became too much. Whatever the case, he put an end to it.

When someone dies, our landscape changes and has to be learnt again. We can no longer think of him in his house or garden, someone to drop in on for a chat, someone to count on, a house you'll leave in the late evening with a bag of books. Everything will change: his library, even his house may disappear to make way for a block of apartments, in the way each generation thinks it is the one that gets things right.

If and when that happens, the warm wind will no longer blow through their fig trees, spreading lovely perfume in warm weather. There will be nothing and no one to remember all of us gathered around a table of fresh breakfast baguettes slathered with the pale sweetness of her fig jam.

-Mary Byrne

REVIEW

what she holds
by d. ellis phelps
moonshadowsanctuarypress
ISBN 9798672793627
Paperback, 120 pgs

As editor of Moon Shadow Sanctuary Press and of fws: international journal of literature and art, Phelps knows well how to turn a phrase. Her poetry collection *what she holds* will likely deliver a sense of retribution for any reader who stems from an abusive family. The author presents herself as one who has witnessed her mother's abuse and suffered her own, at her father's hand.

Phelps offers the title of her collection and each poem in lower case. To convey her pained message, she uses effective visual and poetic devices: spatial separations on the printed page, the forward slash, the tilde, the em dash, varied indentations, italicizations, caesurae, and fragmented phrases. Her concern for meter takes second place to the delivery of her message. Her titles and use of metaphors clearly indicate the interruption she experienced at the death of her father, to whom she dedicated this collection.

The first poem, "uninvited," in the opening section is representative of the collection, particularly in its layout and fragmentations. Descriptions of the father / daughter relationship leave no doubt about the dysfunctions within the family and regrettably indicate unresolved flaws in the relationship after the father's death. The poem, "uninvited," exhibits fear, loss, regret, and desire. It is addressed to the very father who has incited the family pain. On a visit home, the daughter having matured into womanhood, suffers the father's comment, "you're getting fat." Her response follows:

i do not know this

      but we are

making:
>   *transformative soup*

The daughter sees the father's disgust as an "alchemical
fire" of condemnation. This phrase is a fine metaphor
for the abuses she has experienced.

Though I read the volume seated in brightest sunshine,
the darkness of Phelps' imagery threatened to overcome
the light. On page 42, the child is at the feet of her father
who has slammed the head of her mother against the
clapboard, "please please / Daddy please."

In her fourth section "what the darkness hid," the poet
gives further testimony to the abuse. Her poems' titles
are adequate descriptors: "the nights too long," "singe,"
and "first memory."

At page 92, a new confidence, with its hint at optimism,
steps into Phelps' white-spaced scenes:

i know   my place
it has no   walls

& i know

how to keep

what Is mine

The poem, "hold this" follows the above lines and opens
Phelps' final segment entitled "before the crushing." This
poem is an inquiry into the deeper nature of her father,
perhaps at an earlier time in his life. The author searches
for the man "who let go / of the reins / & slept // know-
ing / his horse// would carry him / home" She'd like to
know the father at the time he was such a trusting man.

In "the shaman said," a poem that runs across eight
pages, we witness again the vulnerable child who paid

164

the heavy price of damage to her physical and emotional being, though she tells it slant through the shaman's voice: "how trying / not to drop / the eggs / (you would / be whipped / if you did) / you failed / to catch / your fall / how this / incident / shaped / shifted / you (p. 109)

Later, in the same poem, we find "everything / adding up / —except us" Witness the bite in that final "except us." In spite of this, the shaman advises: "*honor / your ancestor.*" And the poet declares:

to this day
the scent

of sweet

smoke

takes me
home

to you

Readers must trust that the facing of the injurious one is the action that brings the healing. Whether you are fond of confessional poetry, or not, Phelps' arrangement of words brings its own rewards to the attentive reader, whether we name it an "amalgam / —mining gold" or "hand hewn / open mouthed," (p.82) to borrow phrases from the poet. (See "rare flesh" on p.79)

Throughout, Phelps' message and her grasping for reconciliation resounds. In her Afterword, Phelps calls on us to be mirrors for one another, to choose compassion, and to practice forgiveness. That message works well for this reader.

- Carole Mertz

REVIEW

Alexandra and the Awful, Awkward, No Fun, Truly Bad Dates
story by Rebekah Manley, illustrations by Catarina Olivera
Ulysses Press
ISBN 978-1-64604-066-7

Manley's debut Adult Picture Book *Alexandra and the Awful, Awkward, No Fun, Truly Bad Dates* is a fantastic parody that shows the true lows of modern online dating while teaching the reader an important lesson on self-acceptance.

Each experience is told through short, pun-filled sentences, and we join Alexandra as she attempts a "30 dates in 30 days" challenge that helps wheedle out the true crazies from the world of online dating. From a modern-day Mama's Boy to the inevitable no-show, Alexandra uses her 30 days to narrow down what she is truly looking for both in a companion and in life. The ups and downs (mostly downs) of her dating experience brings into light the same questions single adults today have about how far they are willing to compromise to find a partner in life. Her 30-date conclusion is an eye-opening experience that ends happily with Alexandra embracing her own self-love and living life on her own terms, without the validation of having a companion.

Paired with art by Catarina Oliveira, *Alexandra and the Awful, Awkward, No Fun, Truly Bad Dates* flows though the pages of this short book in simple yet bold color. The illustrations enhance the story without over-shadowing the plot. This debut story will have readers laughing out loud at the bizarre yet relatable dating disasters and really connecting with the idea of self-validation and self-acceptance that present itself at the end. *Alexandra* is a book for anyone who has had an online dating experience, or known anyone who has ever dated online.

- Jerica Glover

Contributors

Denise Alden, Eagan, MN.

Christine Andersen, Storrs Mansfield, CT

Lesley Bannatyne, Somerville, MA: Halloween Nation (2020)

J A Bernstein Hattiesburg, MI: Rachel's Tomb (2019), Desert Castles (2019)

Jennifer Bowen Neergaard, Irvington, NY

Wendy Brown-Baez Columbia Heights, MN: Catch a Dream (2020), Heart On the Page (2018)

Mary Byrne, Montpellier, France: Plugging the Causal Breach (2019)

Ron Dowell, Compton, CA

Jordan Escobar, Jamaica Plain, MA

Roberta Gates, Riverside, IL

Jerica Glover, Temple TX

Joan Halperin, Canton, MA

Don Hogle, New York, NY: Madagascar (2020)

Nancy Jorgenson, Waukesha, WI: Go, Gwen, Go (2019)

Gerald Kamens, Falls Church, VA

Kaitlin Kan, Villanova, PA: her debut publication!

Ellaraine Lockie, Sunnyvale, CA: The Gourmet Paper Maker (2001), Wild As In Familiar (2011)

Linda Murphy Marshall, Columbia, MD

Kathleen McGuire, Saint Petersburg, FL

Carole Mertz Parma OH. Color and LIne (2021), Toward a Peeping Sunrise (2019)

Lee Nash, Poitou-Charentes, France: Ash Keys (2017)

Peter Newall, Odessa, Ukraine

Melissa Nunez, Mission, TX

Alan Perry, Maple Grove, MN: Clerk of the Dead (2020)

Barry Peters, Durham, NC

Lisa Poulson, San Francisco, CA

Gary Powell, Cornelius, NC: Lucky Bastard (2011) Super Blood Wolf Moon (2020)

Christina Robertson, Evanston, IL

Lauren Schenkman, New York

Daryl Scroggins, Marfa, TX: Winter Investments (2003), This Is Not the Way We Came In (2009)

Rie Sheridan Rose, Austin TX: The Conn-Mann Chronicles (series)

Harvey Silverman, Manchester, NH

Annette Sisson, Brentwood, TN: A Casting Off (2019)

David Stromberg, Jerusalem, Israel: A Nation Wrongs Itself (2020), Grilled Bananafish (2020)

Ingrid Taylor, Las Vegas, NV

Emily Tobias, Dana Point, CA

Ronald Deane Watson, Madisonville, KY

Manning Wolfe, Austin TX: Dollar Signs (2016), Music Notes (2017), Green Fees (2018)